SEXTETTE

A Romantically Queer Novel in Three Acts

By

A.Y. Caluen

SEXTETTE

Cover design by RK Young

Cover image by Leonard Cotte *unsplash.com*

SEXTETTE

Contents

SEXTETTE

OVERTURE
In which we meet Our Actors On a Rainy Day in 1905

Elizabeth Bonner

Our rooms at the hotel were sufficiently commodious that we might all have been quite private. After the long and tedious ocean crossing, packed into one stateroom and two small cabins, one might have thought we'd want time to ourselves. Instead we huddled together on the bed in my room, determinedly not looking out the window at a gray and rainy early-summer day in London.

"I will ask you again, from time to time," I said. A glance to my right at my steward Marius; one to my left at my dresser Daisy. "If on due consideration you abhor the Old World, I shall send you back to New York. Or wherever you like."

"Never again," Marius said, with feeling. "The Atlantic may heave without me."

Daisy snickered. "You know all our friends are dying to hear of our great adventure. And they all say, give it a year."

Mine – the few true friends I'd left behind, rather than bringing with me – had said the same. England is different, they said; no one will know you there. As if that were a bad thing.

"At least we know already that one thing was true," I said after a moment. "The city is as diverse as New York. No one will look twice at you."

"They'll look twice at *you*, once they know your man of business is black."

Daisy reached across me to pat Marius. "And me."

I made an irritated noise. "I am confident that the people with whom I would choose to be friends will think nothing of it." And oh, how exciting that thought was. I'd crossed the ocean for many reasons; chief among them was to meet someone. All was possibility, and nothing was at stake. I would stay regardless of the outcome, freed by distance from the oversight of my remaining family and the stifling rules of my youth.

Suddenly restless, I kissed Daisy, then Marius. "Up and away, my loves. Let's ring for –"

"Coffee," they said together.

George Fairchild

I poked my head into the library, saw my secretary Inigo where I expected him, and said, "Tea?"

"Gracias," he said absently, attention remaining on the papers before him. Apparently he was in a Spanish mood. That suited me; the day was gray, wet, and chill; to be reminded of more Southern climes was no hardship.

"In the conservatory?"

He looked up then, smiling at me. "Have you turned on the radiator?"

"Naturally. Meet me there?"

"I'll be along shortly, Duchess."

I clicked my tongue at him in mock reproof. After all these years, and especially now that my title was a simple artifact, for him to use it was mere habit. Then I left him, found one of my plentiful staff and gave my order, and wandered off to my conservatory.

This house was my haven, my refuge, and on some days my prison. The late Duke Alfred and I had lived here most of the time when we were in England, though the family seat lay elsewhere. It was far enough distant from the rest of the family that we could be private, near enough to Oxford that we could be on a train within hours at need.

Privacy is a ruling principle when your household is arranged for the comfort of an inverted Duke, his thirty-years-younger and Platonically-devoted bride, and his longtime lover. Neither Inigo nor I would ever stop missing Freddy. At least I'd had a companion the past several years.

I missed Caroline with particular intensity that day. I'd been reading an account, from America, of developments in powered flight. Having traveled (I use the term loosely) by balloon (a chancy and little-controllable endeavor) on several occasions, the prospect of being able to steer one's vehicle aloft, and choose one's landing site, gave me some exciting ideas. She'd been with me for one of those balloon ascensions. I had no doubt that she'd've stood by smiling, though stoically anticipating my imminent fiery demise, as I attempted one of the new machines.

It was too soon to seek a new companion; not too soon to wish for one. England had felt too small for me for years, and I longed to leave it again, but not alone. "There will be someone," I said under my breath, then filled my lungs with the warm, steamy, fragrant air of the conservatory. The orange trees were blooming.

Donald Richards

"This is the sort of day when one prefers Oxford," I told my friend Walpole as we trudged down the mucky London pavement. We were crowded under his umbrella, jostling our way from his house to the nearest pub.

He gave me a sideways look. “No doubt it’s raining there as well.”

Ah, but in Oxford I’d be alone and thus free to stay indoors. Brew a pot of tea over my spirit lamp, turn up the reading lamp, drape a blanket around my shoulders, and lose myself in a book. “How goes your practice these days?”

“Well.” He stood back as I pulled open the pub door, then we lurched inside. His umbrella joined the mob dripping in the vestibule, and we turned toward the taproom. “I’ve acquired a new client with interests in Wales,” he added as we found a table.

“Ooh! Will you travel there?”

“Very shortly. Have you been?”

“Two summers ago, for a ramble in Snowdonia.” Shortly after his wedding, though I did not say so. I’d already heard enough about that, about his wedding trip to Brighton, about settling into the terraced house in Camden. Envy did not suit me. I turned my gaze to the slate above the bar. “Oh my oath, they’ve pork pie and cream o’ leek soup.”

“I’ll have it,” he said, as pleased as I was. Walpole’s wife was away this weekend, so we were obliged to feed ourselves. It was not, strictly speaking, a cold day, but leek soup suited every weather, and a pint or two in a pub always went down well with a slab of pie. “Margaret was sorry to miss you.”

That might’ve been true; we all got on. “She’s well, I trust?”

“Very well.” Now would be the time for him to tell me if they were expecting a child; since he said nothing more, I deduced that they were not. Yet. He changed the subject, in any case, to the much-discussed new Aliens Act. Neither of us had any good to say of it; we had Jewish friends in common. Royal assent seemed a certainty, which meant those friends and their families would be made to feel even less like valued citizens. We cheerfully abused the Act and its perpetrators through the first pint and the pie.

At length, the subject changed to my practice. "I'll never be rich," I said, "but I'm my own man."

"Good feeling, eh?" I nodded. Walpole sat back and eyed me. "D'you think you might marry?"

Oh *damn* the man, why must he ask? It was so unlikely that I'd achieve the necessary security in time to make good use of it. I shrugged, affecting disinterest. "Perhaps I'll acquire a particularly profitable client soon, and the means to house a wife as handsomely as you." He looked pleased at that. I changed the subject again.

Aurelia Dashwood

It was another tedious day of pretending to find my young charge's wardrobe a topic of fascination. She was an appealing-enough young person, but with a Season at last in her sights her attention to my areas of expertise had waned. She'd put up her hair last winter; in the next few months, she would make occasional forays to carefully-selected and scrupulously-supervised social events. I was aware, though not yet on notice, that as of next spring, my services as governess would no longer be required.

In the meantime, I had a pleasant place to live; a summer in the country to enjoy; and a winter of mostly-congenial activity to anticipate. It was no true hardship to accompany a fledgling as she stretched her wings. I might even secure my next post before the end of this one.

A governess is neither fish nor fowl, but I'd acquired a certain expertise in negotiating my place in a house. Thus I was present when the servants convened in the kitchen for tea. Amidst the rambling chatter, the senior footman nodded at me and asked, "What do you do between posts?"

"I've options," I said briskly. "I could go home to my parents. Or I could take lodgings in any city with an employment agency."

"Why would you not go home?"

This from a curious housemaid. I turned to smile at her. "My father's a vicar with a living not far from Brighton. It's a holiday town, and the sort of people who might hire a governess only go there on holiday. I was in London when I secured this post, and my first. The others came by referral."

"What about marriage?" That impertinent question was from the under-footman, several years my junior and a bit of a flirt.

I smiled at him too, concealing the twinge the question cost me. Under no circumstances would I tell these people – friendly, but not my true friends – my whole history. "That is, my dear Wallace, another argument in favor of London."

Cook snorted out a laugh, which reminded us all that she'd met her spouse in the great City. "You can find anything in London," she said, tipping me the wink.

Let it be so, I thought, and raised my cup to her.

Severin LaSalle

I supervised the transfer of my luggage to a sturdy coach, then turned for one last look at the ship. The cabin steward who'd enlivened several of my nights on board was nowhere in sight. We'd said our goodbyes the day before, in a friendly manner that did not preclude my offering a hearty tip. He had, after all, kept my cabin in good order throughout the voyage from Ceylon.

The day was not conducive to bright expectations. After four and a half decades in the tropics, I was well used to rain; but *my* rain came in sheets, followed by hot sun to steam off the wet. *This* rain drizzled, dashing under my hat brim and my jacket with each gust of chill wind off the Thames, promising that I should be permanently cold here. I cast one more assessing glance over the load, then hauled my shivering self up into the coach.

Bright expectations or not, I had much business to transact here in England. My relations (most notably a Marquess based in Yorkshire) would soon see my face for the first time. It was, in fact, the first time any of my branch of the family had come to England since my ancestor left it over a hundred years before. Before he died, my father told me I should come. "I might have gone," he said. "Might've applied to have the title restored. You might be a baronet after me."

I'd stared at him, saying nothing; after a moment, we'd both burst out laughing. What did we want with an English title?

Our family's history was a matter of hundreds of pages of parchment, laboriously kept, expanded by each LaSalle when something of particular note occurred. I brought with me a clean copy; one of my aims was to arrange for its publication.

The name would die with me. Before that happened, I hoped to change my life. If all went well with my cousin, management of the estate would pass to my sister, and thence to her children. I would be free.

For a man of my age, who might reasonably be looking forward to retirement from decades of work, to be wishing rather to start over might be odd. My education and my business experience could open new doors for me, if I made the right friends here or on the Continent.

To also make the sort of friends who'd enliven my leisure was a wish that might not come to fruition. I would have less freedom for such things here. At best I might find temporary solace.

In, all the gods willing, a warm room.

Inigo Salazar

I joined Fairchild in the conservatory, tugging at my cravat to loosen it. She'd told me a hundred times that I need not dress formally at home, but after a half-century I had the habit of it. A suit and tie were, in a sense, my armor: a reminder that while she was my friend, she was also my employer, and that this was my home only by her gift.

"You are pensive today," I remarked after we'd made inroads on our first cups of tea. "Something troubling you?"

"Not to say troubled. I was reading about the Wright brothers in America and their mad venture with motorized aircraft."

"Oh, God, and I suppose you want one. I'm constantly amazed you haven't acquired a motorcar." She laughed. I smiled into my teacup. Sipped again, then set it aside and reached for a biscuit. Raised my eyebrows at her.

She sighed. “I’m restless.”

“Of course you are.”

“This time of year, I’m usually planning an adventure. Or at least an excursion. But since Caroline.” Her voice trailed off.

I reached over to pat her arm. “A few more months. Then no one will make a scene if you begin living a full life again.” Mourning needn’t last forever, though in my case I often wondered if it would. Where would I ever find someone to fill the hole left in my heart by losing Freddy? Did I even want to? I dismissed the thought. “To the world, she was only your companion.”

Fairchild sniffed dismissively. Ate a biscuit, drank some tea, then leaned back in her rattan chair and tipped her head up. The palm tree towering above us was quivering in the faint breeze drifting through an open casement. Some local birds (the reason for the open casement) had a nest in a crevice where an old petiole had been cut away. “D’you suppose they find mates more easily because their lives are short?”

A philosophical question, to which I returned a provocative answer. “Because they have no religion.”

She laughed again, sprawling in the chair, expression lighter than I’d seen it in months. “Ah, God, Inigo. What would I do without you.”

“The question is not likely to arise,” I said with composure, freshening my cup. Making eye contact as she straightened, wordlessly communicating two facts: I had already more joy in life than most men of my sort could even imagine; she was now the person who knew me best, and loved me best, in all the world.

I could not wish for more.

Now enter upon

THE EMERALD BOA

Featuring an American Coquette,
an Aristocratic Lady, and
A Stolen Artifact

Elizabeth

George Fairchild was the sort of person who defies categorization. In certain circles, Fairchild was known as a crack shot, a bruising rider, a fair boxer, and a deadly *artiste* of the saber. In others, as a fine scholar, a dashing explorer, and a captivating chronicler of adventures far beyond the Empire. To more conventional members of society, Fairchild was a scandal, an outrage, and a disgrace to her family.

Yes: *her* family. She once said if it was good enough for Middlemarch, it was good enough for her.

Fairchild could order a meal or haggle for a horse in seven or eight languages and curse you in as many more. She'd traveled around the world by the age of twenty-five and published six books by thirty. She was a bit of a legend in Oxford, and even I, from my apartment on Fifth Avenue, had heard of her before I attained my independence.

Which, by the way, was a damned long time coming.

I finally met Fairchild in the summer of 1905, having traveled by steamer from New York for the express purpose of making her acquaintance. Matters of business kept me in London longer than I liked, but I met an extraordinary number of people, many of whom I did like; and at length I was away. I traveled by train to Oxford, put up in a respectable inn, and sent around my card with a request for an audience.

A response came from her secretary: *The Duchess is not receiving due to her recent loss. She thanks you for your kind indulgence.*

Had I not mentioned that? George Fairchild, at all of eighteen, became the bride of the Duke. Now (and five years past) the late Duke. His heir is, according to my new friend Donald, very bitter concerning the terms of the will. At any rate, I was at a standstill. What loss?

I sent immediately for a contact of mine in the City, a young solicitor who I felt would surely be able to inform me. He joined me for dinner, and did so inform me. "The Duchess' cousin, Lady Caroline Paget, succumbed to influenza four months ago. Lady Caroline was the Duchess' companion these last six years; they were very close."

Hmm. Companion, very close: there were several possible interpretations. "How unfortunate. And how gauche of me; surely I ought to have known this."

"Perhaps those you saw in London were not aware. The Duchess has never spent much of her time in town."

I shrugged it off. "It doesn't matter. Maybe you can help me in another way. I have left America, you see, with the intention of settling in England. Can you advise me as to how I might go about hiring a house here in Oxford?"

"I should be happy to, Miss Bonner."

"Thank you, Mr. Walpole."

Along with setting certain legal matters in motion, Mr. Walpole referred me to a local associate, a Mr. Donald Richards, who delighted me by betraying no discomposure at the notion of an unmarried American woman of means making herself at home in the city of dreaming spires. A series of dinners and teas and property viewings followed this meeting, ending six weeks later with the purchase (not lease; after viewing the typical contract I decided a landlord was undesirable) of an early-Victorian house a furlong from the Cherwell. It took another two weeks to render the place sufficiently habitable (I make no apology for high standards), and yet two more for the remainder of my luggage to arrive from its warehouse in London. Donald, at the end of a friendly evening (it began with dinner, progressed to an earnest attempt to teach me to play chess, and on to – well, I draw the veil of discretion here), suggested my steward Marius should drop in to the Equatorial Club to see about a housekeeper, et cetera.

By the time the house was properly furnished, Marius and I had engaged a cook-housekeeper, Miss Ashvi Gould; a groom-driver, Mr. Sam Darley; and a maid-of-all-work, Miss Mary Johnson. Ashvi and my dresser Daisy negotiated the division of labor; Sam procured a carriage horse and vehicle, as well as a mannerly retired steeplechaser for me to ride; Mary wasted no time putting the walled garden at the southeast corner of the house to rights. It was a flurry of activity such as I had not seen since my father died.

At the expiration of this period, Donald informed me that he had learned, via the village telegraph as it were, that the dowager Duchess of --- was now receiving. I lost no time in sending around my card again. This time I received a far more encouraging reply: *The Duchess would be pleased to make the acquaintance of Miss Elizabeth Bonner on the afternoon of --- . If this date is acceptable, no reply is necessary.*

The date was, needless to say, acceptable.

When I reached the estate – it was a smashing ride out from Oxford; my new horse (which someone had fancifully named Wellington) was a joy – I slowed so that I could take in the grounds. I'd heard that the

Duchess let the place go wild; to my American eyes, it was nothing of the sort. Indeed, it was like a very well-groomed park. Perhaps they meant the lack of topiary? The absence of follies? The fox perched on a low wall, observing the passing rider with what can only be described as a smug expression? Wide riding paths, and shaded walking paths, with sturdy bridges over a stream that wound through the park: I thought it lovely.

Dismounting at the front door, I was greeted by an astounding butler. His manner was impeccable and his livery superb; the man himself was nearly seven feet tall, and dark as a glass of Guinness. After I presented my calling card, he gestured me in with a regal bow.

The receiving hall was a perfectly symmetrical cube. The great double front door was echoed by another pair of doors straight ahead, through which I could see the base of a staircase. To the right and left were archways defined by elaborate moldings, each framed by a brace of tall mirrors. Under each mirror stood a japanned cabinet holding a wide, low dish containing a blooming orchid. The floor was of marble, inlaid with a compass rose; in the center of the ceiling was a Venetian chandelier, hanging from a gilded medallion. I caught tantalizing glimpses of the rooms to each side before the butler ushered me through the second set of double doors.

I thought at first I would be conveyed up the stairs ahead; instead, we turned left and went down a short hall.

"The ladies' retiring room, Miss," quoth the butler, indicating a door to our right. We went on, past what was clearly a library, and moreover one that I craved much more than a glimpse of, eventually fetching up at French doors leading into a conservatory. The butler opened these doors and bowed me in. "Miss Bonner, your grace," he intoned. I looked around, but could see no one.

"Thank you, Amon. Come forward six paces, Miss Bonner," said a disembodied voice. I observed the butler's silent exit, then obeyed. "Now turn right." I did. She was standing on a ladder with her back to me, shears in hand, doing something to an exotic plant clinging to the side of a palm tree.

"Good afternoon, your grace. Thank you for seeing me."

She glanced over her shoulder. "I'll be finished in a moment. There's a lounge area another six paces ahead. I'll join you there."

"All right." I went forward, marveling at the tropical jungle around me. Palm, banana, and citrus trees filled the space; interspersed were tables bearing more orchids. The air was warm and humid. I could swear I heard the hiss of a snake and the chirp of birds. The hiss I later determined to be the voice of a steam radiator; the birds were real, coming and going through a half-open casement.

I was standing alongside a lavishly-set refreshment table when the Duchess reached me, wiping her hands with a large and vividly-printed calico handkerchief. She held out her hand; I took it; we shook. Then I completely embarrassed myself. "I've been longing to meet you ever since I read your first book."

She raised an eyebrow. "You must have been in the nursery yet." Her voice was low and well-modulated, with crisp diction and a warmth of humor.

"I'm twenty-five. And three-quarters."

"A good age. Have you been to England before?"

"No; in fact I have never been outside America before."

"Well, I am honored to be part of your first tour abroad. Please sit. You rode out today."

"Yes." I was removing my hat and gloves as she spoke, laying them aside. Wearing my new and very daring habit (I much preferred to ride astride, so this bore a closer resemblance to a gentleman's riding costume than to a fashionable lady's habit) had been less of a risk with this particular noblewoman than with any of the others I'd yet met. Indeed, her expression was approving.

"Would you prefer tea, coffee, or something stronger?"

"I do not, I confess, much care for tea; and I need to keep my wits about me. Coffee, please."

She made an amused sound and poured for both of us. I studied her with frank interest. The illustrations in her books had given me a general impression, but in person she was much more striking. She was tall and slim; today she wore tweed trousers and vest with a white shirt, sleeves rolled up to show strong, tanned forearms and graceful but not at all dainty hands. Her straight fawn hair was cut short. At a distance, especially if she wore a student gown, one would take her for a young man. At close range, one saw the fine lines at her eyes and mouth, betraying years in the outdoors. The smooth, narrow jaw and slender neck had never known a razor. Yet I could see how she had traveled unmolested for so long, in so many hazardous places. There was nothing feminine about her. Dressed as a man, armed, and carrying herself as she did: one's first impression (and probably tenth) would not lead one to 'proper young lady.' Rather might one think 'Allan Quatermain's younger brother.' Her eyes were large, blue-gray, deep-set, and fringed with straight lashes under equally straight and uncompromising brows. She was quite splendid. She was also studying me with equivalent interest.

"I perceive that you know somewhat about me, Miss Bonner. Tell me a bit about yourself. How come you to travel alone to England?"

"I attained my independence upon my last birthday, your grace."

"For God's sake, call me Fairchild."

The smile that went with that – ooh! I swallowed and went on. "Then I beg you will call me Elizabeth. What was I – oh yes. Till recently I was living in New York in the apartment left me by my grandfather. Thaddeus Bonner."

"I know the name, but its significance escapes me."

"He was a country lawyer, but he happened to own a large tract of land through which Mr. Carnegie proposed to route his railroad." This was not the whole truth of my family, nor the whole source of my financial well-being, but it was (I thought) sufficient unto the day.

"Ah, indeed. The history of the railroads is the history of the industrial revolution. One cannot imagine, nor fully appreciate, the modern world without the railroads. May I ask the derivation of your name?"

"It is from the French. Bonheur."

"A fine name; one cannot wish more than happiness."

Her tone prompted me to say, "I was very sorry to hear of your recent loss, Y- Fairchild. Please accept my sympathies."

"Thank you; Lady Caroline was very dear to me. And I have not yet forgiven her for leaving me without a companion for my further adventures."

"May I ask where you propose to travel next?"

"As yet undetermined." This was clearly a cause of discontent. She leaned back in her chair – sprawled, rather, in a way that was unspeakably alluring – and stared at me. "How do you find your new house?"

I blinked, somewhat startled by this change of subject, and slightly unnerved. I had not expected the Duchess to have any interest in me, much less to have made any inquiries. But, after all, Oxford was a small town. No doubt a high tide of gossip was produced by the luminous moon of a newcomer. "I am assured that we sit above the flood plain; my staff mostly come from the Equatorial Club; the kitchen garden was a wilderness; and the stable appeared to have been tenanted by nothing more than pigeons, rats, and the occasional fox for decades. However, with the aid of a terrier, and some day help of the human variety, we have remedied the ravages of neglect and are nearly ready to entertain."

"And is that the point of residing in Oxford?"

Good gracious, what a tone. Distinctly sardonic. Well, what did she know of me, after all, except that I rode astride and hired people without regard to skin color. Both of which she did herself. I tilted my head a few degrees and narrowed my eyes. "The point of residing in Oxford is, first, to make your acquaintance."

Her eyes narrowed too, in a way that had nothing of annoyance about it. "And second?"

"To be *perfectly* frank, I hope to inveigle my way into the Bodleian. If I cannot do that, I intend to engage a tutor and begin filling in the woeful gaps in my education." I composedly drank the rest of my coffee and set down the Limoges cup. Folded my hands in my lap and gave her what I very much hoped was a persuasive smile. "There is no reason for me ever to return to America. My steward and dresser would prefer never to set foot on a trans-Atlantic vessel again. The largest room in my house is meant for a library. Family history suggests I have at least fifty years ahead in which to stuff my brain full of all the things the world does not care to teach women."

"Oh, Elizabeth."

Great Scott, the caressing tone of that voice. The warm smile, the – *ooh.* I opened my mouth to say something less personal. Instead what came out was, "The last thing I want is to go back and marry one of the buffoons my aunts were continually parading before me."

She laughed. Oh God, I was utterly sunk.

Fairchild

"I am utterly sunk."

The laugh from Inigo would have offended a lesser woman. I flung myself into my desk chair and stared broodily at him. "You knew she was unusual," he said, undisturbed, reaching for his tin of pipe tobacco. "A Radcliffe graduate."

"Be damned to that," I growled enviously. "She is the most brazen, beguiling, enticing bit of baggage ever to have crossed my path. Rode up – unaccompanied, if you please – on that fine old 'chaser of Lord Robert's, kitted out like a mistress of hounds. I'd like to shake her tailor's hand." The truth was, I'd like to do considerably more than that. It was a surprise, equal parts delightful and unsettling. Losing Caroline had left me bereft in more ways than one, but I was rarely attracted to someone I'd just met. However, that part of my life was one of the few in which Inigo was not involved, so I changed the subject. "Find out who she's hired, would you? She wants access to the Library. Failing that, as she surely will, a tutor. You might know someone who would mesh with her household."

Inigo knew everyone in the 'educated sort employed (or aspiring to be) by cultured gentry' category. He also knew that if we could provide the ideal party, Miss Bonner would be obliged to me, which was exactly my aim. "All right. What else can I do for you today?"

I had nothing to do, and we both knew it. I'd been considering London. My club there would have room for me; I could see some of my itinerant friends, write letters to others, visit the British Museum. Fill the time. I sighed. "Any interesting letters? Or anything in the papers?"

He made a noncommittal sound that got my attention. "Bit of scandal in Belgravia."

"What sort of scandal?"

"Shouting match at the residence of Sir Leighton Cavill. Person dressed as a tradesman, or clerk – depending on the witness – scuffling with a footman on the doorstep. The words 'you're a bloody thief' were heard."

"Cavill." Why did I know that name?

"Whose sister is believed to have been the model for Beryl Stapleton in a certain sensational serial in The Strand." He said that with sibilant glee; the man adored all things Sherlock Holmes.

"Oh! Crikey!" I sat up straight. "I say, that *is* a scandal. What do we know about the sister?"

"Very little, beyond widowhood due to unknown and thus highly suspicious circumstances. If the story has any basis in fact, her husband used her most wretchedly. And, no doubt, her family would have had nothing more to do with her. Shall I investigate?"

"No," I said, mind racing. "I will." This was the perfect excuse for a London sojourn. I could take my ease with a person whom I'd not seen in years but knew to be congenial, brush up my fencing, harass my friend Tom at Scotland Yard, and uncover the truth underlying 'The Hound of the Baskervilles.' It would be a great frolic, exactly what I needed to keep my mind off a certain young American. An American who might be beguiling but whom I could not expect to be congenial in the way I wished. Despite the intriguing way she responded to my louche behavior. *You are a cad, George Fairchild.* The thought made me smile.

Then I looked across the room at Inigo, calmly lighting his pipe. I loved him almost as much as I'd loved Freddy, and had no wish to do without him, but it was time to ask again. "Are you content, amigo? Any wish to return to Madrid?" I meant 'to live,' rather than 'to visit.'

He gazed at me steadily through the smoke. How I adored his blend, the sweet weight of it in the air. "There is little for me in Spain, Duchess. And Freddy wanted me to look after you."

"All you've done the past quarter-century is look after Fairchilds. If not Spain, the south of France. Jamaica. California?"

My skeptical tone made him laugh. "The Gold Rush is over, my dear, and I am too old to travel." I snorted at that; he was only fifty. His fine eyes flashed with amusement. "Your household suits me. My occupation is congenial. I have old friends here with whom I may reminisce, and new friends ready to hand."

He meant that literally, as I well knew. The Equatorial Club was many things. A lodging house, an employment bureau, and a discreet place of assignation for those whose meetings were of a nature not readily accommodated elsewhere. Inigo had been Freddy's lover for thirteen years before I entered the picture, and no doubt would be still, had the Duke's horse not taken a fence wrong. I would be the last person to say he should not now seek companionship where he could. With that in mind, I returned to our previous topic. "I'll go down to London tomorrow. Put up at the Boudica for a few days and see what I can discover about Sir Leighton and the bloody thief."

"Sounds like a yellow-back title," Inigo murmured.

"Our favorite genre." I bared my teeth in a smile, heaved myself out of the chair, and went to ruin Polly's day.

My dresser set her underlings scurrying as she peppered me with irritated questions. "To London on half a day's notice? For how long? For what purpose?"

"Yes, I don't know, nothing formal. I've no intention of dining anywhere but at the club or in seedy taverns. But if I have to pay a call in Belgravia, I'd best have the blue serge." There were occasions, mostly in London, when I bowed to convention and wore skirts. My compromise was to have them made of menswear fabrics. The blue serge was a practical costume comprising a full skirt and fitted jacket. I typically wore it with a white shirtwaist, a Liberty tie, sturdy boots and a jaunty hat.

"You'll have the gray as well," Polly instructed me. "And a *proper* dinner dress. You might order something new for the holidays. The invitations will start coming soon."

"The holidays? It's high summer!"

"Yes, but for all anyone knows you'll be off again out of England any day now."

I might have been, too, if not for the twin mysteries of the bloody thief and Miss Bonner.

The next day Polly, my trunk, and I were conveyed to the train station and thence to London. The rest of the household were glad to see the back of me. A hired carriage delivered me to my club in ample time to unpack, call down for a bottle of dry sherry, and fossick through a bin of correspondence. I generally got down to London once a month or so, but since Caroline's funeral had been sulking at home. Or, to call it what it was, mourning. Our relationship had been close. And it was too blasted soon to lose another person I cared for. Losing Freddy had nearly flattened me. If the horse hadn't been destroyed in the field, I might well have done it myself.

As usual, I instructed myself to buck up and take it like a man. Meaning stiff upper lip, nose in the air, calm demeanor. That nearly fell apart after dinner, when my friend Sybil flung herself into the chair beside mine in the library. "George! As I live and breathe! I'd begun to think we wouldn't see you at all this year."

"It's only a few months since I buried Lady Caroline," I reminded her, a bit tetchily. "Why are you in London?"

"Because my husband can't speak of anything but the hunt and the harvest. I'm bored to sobs. How long are you here?"

I shrugged. "A few days. Have you seen Amelia?"

"Yes, we went to the theatre last night. She asked after you."

"Did she." I suppressed a smile. "I'll send round a card."

"Are you planning a new adventure?" That conversation went on through a glass of Madeira (for Sybil), a glass of Glenfiddich (for me), and a plate of cake (for each of us). Then she said, "If you'd care to join me at home tomorrow evening, there's a new gentleman in town who's set all the ladies a-flutter. It's time you should consider a new husband and I think you'd find him interesting."

I stared at her. Only the fact that Sybil was a true and good friend kept me from releasing any of the hot words piling up in my throat. Instead of speaking, I consulted the bottom of my whisky glass.

"Oh dear," she said after a silent minute. "I've put my foot in it. Still, darling? It's five years now."

"I'm aware."

"You did say he was perfect for you, but dearest, you're not too old for children. With another man –"

"Sybil, I beg of you, desist." I couldn't tell her the unvarnished truth, which was that before we even married Freddy and I agreed not to try for children. We adored each other in a perfectly Platonic way. I never wanted to be pregnant, and he was content that his younger brother – who was, at the time I married Freddy, already a husband and the father of a reasonably promising boy – should inherit the title. After a moment I sighed. "I don't wish to marry again, and my books are my children. I will come to dinner if you think this person would amuse me, but I shall come dressed like this." I was wearing tailored trousers and vest, and certainly wouldn't insult her by appearing for dinner in the same, but she took my meaning.

"In other words, govern myself accordingly." To her credit, she was amused. "He'll dine out on the story for as long as he's in England."

"He's welcome to."

"And now I'll leave you in peace before I risk truly offending you. It's lovely to see you, dear. Until tomorrow."

"Tomorrow," I echoed, watching her go. She'd been at my wedding. It was a sensation at the time, of course; Freddy was three decades older than I, and a confirmed bachelor. At least until we met at one of the spring balls. He asked me to dance, with an air of having no expectations. How he loved to dance. A very physical person, was Freddy. Riding, climbing, boxing, fencing, rowing, dancing. Had he been inclined to women, no doubt he would have been a legendary lover.

He also had an adventurous mind. During that first dance, one or the other of us said just the right thing to begin a true conversation. We quickly discovered interests in common, and then a compatible (if somewhat sideways) view of the world. Within weeks we were engaged. My parents didn't even question it. Their odd daughter, snabbling a duke? Who cared that he was old enough to be my father! Our honeymoon was a sailing trip around the world, with a hand-picked crew including my maid and Inigo. Before we were out of sight of land, Inigo knew I'd no desire to evict him from Freddy's bed.

On our return, my maid quit her employment the moment we docked in Plymouth, going home to the Midlands a good deal richer and disinclined to gossip about her employers. Instead she used our letters of reference to secure a position as a matron at a girls' school. I went to London, opened up Freddy's town house, and settled in to write a book. He went home to his primary seat with Inigo. For nine years we shared what to me was a perfect life. A balance of society, study, activity, and adventure. Making appearances at all the essential events, keeping up with estate business, indulging our desires in peace and privacy. Once I found Polly (backstage at the theatre), our four-part conspiracy was secure.

To my knowledge, no one ever questioned the long tenure of Freddy's Spanish secretary. They'd met at The Prado, both attending the opening of a grand exhibition. Freddy had numerous friends among Spanish high society; Inigo was a younger son, with a supportive family but modest prospects. Employment in Spain did not appeal. Secretary to an English Duke, however, was a different matter. Inigo's family saw the post as security for their son and a beneficial connection for them. If they ever suspected that Freddy and Inigo fell headlong into love, they certainly gave no hint of it at our numerous meetings over the years.

Inigo might not want to live there again, but he still had family. Perhaps we should go, for a month or so, after the turn of the year.

I wondered if Miss Bonner would like to see Spain. Miss Bonner, who had during her brief sojourn in London managed to discover the Boudica and write to me here. It seemed she really had been determined to meet me. Her letter was every bit as engaging as the lady in person. The names she dropped – people she must have met for the first time very recently, since she'd not visited England before – were all known to me. Evidently I was not the only one who found the young lady a charming diversion.

Polly was in no mood for me that night, and knew very well that I'd sent a card round to Amelia. We agreed that she should have the next day free to catch up with friends here in town. She suggested I might bestir myself to the acquisition of a new tie to wear with my gray the following night, for dinner at Sybil's. I meekly agreed, told her I needed nothing further, and prepared for bed.

The club was not as luxurious as my own house; the washroom was shared, and located at the end of the hall; but it was laid out with separate rooms for WC, bath, and general ablutions. I washed thoroughly, conscious of the impure city air, then returned down the hall to my rooms. Coal fire banked, dressing gown and slippers off, settled comfortably against the headboard.

Stacked neatly on the bedside table under a steadily-burning gas lamp were the letters I hadn't yet responded to. Among those, Miss Bonner's. As a matter of discipline I took up my fountain pen and made a list of errands to be accomplished in the coming days. Then I selected a fresh sheet of paper.

> Dear Miss Bonner,
>
> Having already made your acquaintance, I was pleased to find your letter awaiting me at the Boudica Club. After several months away I find there are numerous people I should see. No doubt once I begin seeing people, my obligations will proliferate.
>
> Have you yet spoken with the keepers of the library? If the results are not as desired, my secretary (Mr. Salazar) may be able to recommend you a tutor.

In hopes this finds you well.

Yrs – G. Fairchild

I read it over, dissatisfied. Mentioning my obligations was code for 'I'll be in town for a while.' The fact that I wrote at all was an invitation for her to write back. I ought simply have said 'write to me,' but this would have to do.

The following day I knocked out half a dozen of my errands, including a few hours with Amelia which did not go quite as anticipated. She greeted me warmly, wearing a dressing gown over not much else. We talked for a while in the parlor, both expecting to go to bed. We ceased to talk before long, but it was clear that my mind was elsewhere. She sighed, sat back, and stared at me. "George, don't flatter yourself. If I required someone else's hand to ease me I'd've combusted long ago."

I laughed, blushed, and apologized. "I'm truly happy to see you. I've missed your company."

"The same, my dear. Tell me why your mind is so far from my abundant charms."

Of course I ended up telling her all about Miss Bonner, and then about the case of the bloody thief. After that moderately embarrassing interlude I returned to the club to wash and dress for dinner. Polly was in fine fettle, having seen a number of her former associates, and thus full of theatre gossip. She approved of my new Liberty tie (orange butterflies on a navy field, luscious with the gray silk twill) and of the matching silk butterfly for my top hat. Made a non-committal sound when I advised her that I meant to find Agatha Fletcher, née Cavill, the next day. "How d'you plan to manage that?"

"I'll call on Tom Bailey in the morning. The Yard may have taken an interest when her husband died."

"The Inspector will be glad to see you."

I laughed at the sarcasm in her tone. Tom had been a friend of Freddy's – neither of them would tell me how they met, which gave me certain ideas – and was inclined to be scandalized by my unladylike ways. Not so much that he wouldn't have a pint with me from time to time. Polly stood back, smoothing the shoulders of the jacket. "Well enough?"

She fastened a topaz pin in my tie, then stood back. Nodded approval. "You look smashing, love. Make sure that doorman doesn't put you in a dirty cab."

"He knows better." I gave her a kiss. "No need to wait up."

"No intention of it," she said smartly. "I'm off to the Strand."

"Take a cab." She snorted and rolled her eyes, but I knew she'd comply. The days of seeing London from the pavement were long past. "Wish me luck with this colonial friend of Sybil's."

Elizabeth

I was surprised and delighted to receive a letter (however brief) from Fairchild. It might have been simple courtesy; she would surely know that an invitation to tea or dinner would be forthcoming after her kind reception, and this way I would know not to issue such an invitation till she returned to Oxford. On the other hand, she owed me no courtesies. Thus the letter made me feel quite – well, *cozy*, for want of a better word. It was a friendly gesture, and since I'd been regrettably plain about my hero-worship, it told me she was unoffended. And possibly interested. I wrote back promptly regarding unsatisfactory librarians, trying to make a funny story of a demoralizing meeting.

With access to the Bodleian appearing unlikely, I suggested tea (I was coming around to it, thanks to Ashvi's clever hand with spices) with Donald. "What do you advise?"

He stirred thoughtfully. I listened to the faint crunch of sugar crystals and waited with the appearance of patience. After a moment he looked up and said, "There is a man I know to be seeking a post as a tutor. A doctoral candidate, classics and divinity."

"How do you know him?"

"We met in a lecture, and had friends in common. His name is Gould."

"What, like Ashvi?"

"Exactly like; he is her brother."

I may have scowled. Ashvi had never given me to understand she had a single living relative. Donald's alarmed expression caused me to repair my own. "I shall have a word with her about not confessing to family. We ought to have had him to dine by now!"

He opened his mouth to speak and visibly checked himself. A few seconds later, he said, "I could call round at his rooms this afternoon. His porter will take a message if Gould isn't in."

So one thing led to another. I pretended to scold Ashvi about keeping secrets; she pretended to be chastened; a few days later I met her brother. He was … well, suffice it to say he was four years younger than his sister and equally beautiful. Polite, well-spoken, and as affectless as a marble statue until the moment Marius entered the library.

A few words about Marius. He was, like my dresser Daisy, of mixed race. In other words, not a white man. Also like Daisy, he was well-spoken and highly intelligent. He stood nearly six feet tall, his curly black hair gleamed with macassar, and his sharp brown eyes missed nothing about Sunnam Gould.

Marius was probably there out of curiosity; certainly there was nothing I required of him at the moment. In any case I would have sworn I saw a spark leap between them. My people of course were accustomed to complete freedom with me, but Gould wouldn't know that. His initial reaction – a sudden intake of breath, wide eyes, parted lips – passed so quickly it might never have been. Then he blinked, swallowed, and picked up the thread of our conversation. "I would be happy to tutor you in Greek or Latin if you wish, Miss Bonner. Latin in particular may be of use if you intend to study natural history."

"And if I wish to improve my French, no doubt. I've an interest in learning Spanish," I said without much hope. It was unlikely he knew the language.

He shook his head regretfully. "I don't have Spanish myself, but surely we could find you a native speaker through the Equatorial Club."

Or Fairchild's secretary, I thought, stifling a smile. Thanks to Donald and Marius I happened to know that Mr. Salazar was from Madrid. "All in good time," I suggested. "Let us discuss your availability and mine." Another brief reaction, this one of surprise. I knew by now that when someone said they 'read classics' that was exactly what they meant, but there were essays, and meetings with fellow scholars, and interrogations by the masters; he would have fewer hours to spare than I. Evidently he'd thought I would say 'you must be here at specific times.' We cleared that up, negotiated a rate, and shook hands. I sent him on his way and turned to look at Marius.

He'd been standing by the wall of bookshelves, affecting to review the volumes acquired to date. A trunk of books had come with me from New York, and I'd been on a buying spree ever since, but it takes time to fill a proper library. And he had no interest in most of those subjects anyway. He crossed to the door, gently closed it, and said softly, "That's Ashvi's *brother*?"

I nearly giggled. "Mmhmm."

Two weeks later, I'd exchanged several more letters with Fairchild; had several illuminating meetings with Sunnam; hosted a riotous dinner for several new friends from the Equatorial – including Inigo Salazar – and Donald; and begun to pay and return calls. My first dinner invitation had come in, which meant a consultation with Daisy and a local expert to ensure that what I proposed to wear was acceptable. I wanted my hostess to feel ever so slightly superior, as if she were doing me a favor, while at the same time demonstrating perfect fashion sense. Plus, of course, I must look every inch the heiress.

To intentionally display wealth without vulgarity is a challenge. The dress in question was made for me in London, so it was au courant: flowing skirt, short train, flounced hem; low, draped neckline; short sleeves like flower petals; embroidered in plain silk; all in a shade of mild blue that flattered me without being too showy. I wore a suite of pearls, instead of the sapphires I'd worn in London. The results were satisfactory. The evening otherwise was a bit of a chore.

Upon arriving home I went through the door in my usual public way – poised, genteel, orderly – and waited (with, I think, laudable restraint) for Mary to close it behind me before exploding. "Aaaaaugh!"

"Your gloves, miss?" She said it composedly, as if it were completely unremarkable for an ostensibly well-bred young lady to arrive home screaming. I stripped off the gloves and handed them to her. Allowed her to take my cloak and drape it across her arm. "Cup of tea?"

"Thank you Mary, I intend to proceed directly to the nearest decanter. *What* a tiresome evening. Is Marius at home?"

"Yes, miss, but –"

I didn't let her finish, which was rude of me. "I'll find him. You may lock up and be at ease."

"Thank you, miss, but –"

"No, it's quite all right." I smiled absently in her direction and made for the library.

"He's in his room, miss!"

She sounded a bit desperate. So was I; I said "Thank you!" over my shoulder and put my foot on the bottom step.

"Miss, please, Mr. Gould is here!"

That stopped me; I turned. "Is he?"

"Yes, Miss."

"With Mr. Knight, you mean?"

"Yes, Miss."

"Did they dine?"

"Yes, Miss."

"Let me see if I take your meaning, Mary, my dear. Sunnam came for dinner and is now with Marius upstairs, possibly engaged in social activity of a private nature?"

Her eyes went wide; she nodded silently, then cleared her throat. "I could go up first and knock?"

"Darling girl, I shall take *enormous* pleasure in bursting in upon them. If they are only playing cards I shall be greatly disappointed. Have a lovely evening." Oh, I was so mischievous, but the prospect of walking in on Marius and Sunnam in flagrante was so delightful that my entire laborious night's work was quite swept away. I swiftly mounted the stairs, went directly to Marius' bedchamber door, and turned the knob. I do like these, I thought, glancing at the fine Arts and Crafts details on the bronze backplate before pushing the door open. "Oh, *what* a surprise."

"Christ!"

"Lizzie!"

There is no way to convey, in conventional typesetting, the simultaneity of those two exclamations. I smiled blandly at the men as I closed the door behind me. "Good evening gentlemen. No, don't get up. I've only come for a sedative." Such a liar; nearly all the rooms in the house were equipped for that purpose. I crossed to the drinks table and poured myself a finger of whisky, added soda, then turned to consider the occupants of the bed. "You look fetching, Mr. Gould."

A complexion like his or Marius' does not readily betray a blush. The trembling hand holding a cigarette, however, told me Sunnam was either deeply embarrassed or thoroughly terrified, and possibly both. He was sitting up against the headboard, almost-wearing the very fine Scottish paisley robe I'd given Marius for his birthday. His chest was a work of art, not at all what I'd've expected of a scholar. Did he row? I should have to inquire later. I turned my attention to my longtime friend, whose initial startled dismay had given way to frustrated amusement. He reached down for the quilt and tugged it up enough to cover his parts. The rest of him was bare, and a stimulating sight it was. Evidently, in the moment before I opened the door, Marius was lying with his head in Sunnam's lap. Quite sweet, really. I liked to lie thus myself after social activity of a private nature. His expression was reproachful as he assumed something closer to a seated position. "Lizzie, you should knock."

"I knew you were here," I said, meaning both of them, as I plopped down on the bed beside him. "Mary warned me."

"You look marvelous." After a moment to observe me, he said, "I take it your evening out was less than congenial."

"I am fed to the teeth with being spoken to in that insufferably indulgent way. Condescended to. Verbally patted on my empty-by-implication if well-coiffed head, and instructed to direct my attention to a woman's proper place."

"That being to marry some idler and turn all your money and ability over to him?

"Precisely." We'd had this discussion many times before. "Sunnam, may I?" I reached for the cigarette, which he'd forgot to smoke. Before I took a drag, I gulped down the rest of my whisky and tapped the near-to-tumbling ash into the empty glass. Sucked in a burning lungful of smoke, choked, coughed, and dropped the butt in the glass. Marius was laughing. I handed the glass to Sunnam, who placed it on the bedside table. He appeared incapable of speech. Once I'd recovered my breath, I bent down to unbuckle my shoes, kicked them off, and tucked my feet up under my skirts. Patted Marius on his bare leg and left my hand there. "I'll confess I had designs upon you myself tonight, dear, but I won't stay long. Simply seeing you this way has restored my temper."

"Did you learn anything from those people, or did you just reinforce your prejudices?"

That made me laugh. I'm not sure if Sunnam was relaxing, or if he'd simply gone numb. He looked at Marius, who smiled back at him. Sunnam took a visibly-deep breath and turned his gaze to me. "Miss Bonner, I beg your –"

"Don't you think we could dispense with formality? Call me Elizabeth."

"I – I have never – never addressed a lady by her given name."

A white lady, he meant, because I'd heard him call Daisy by her name. "Sunnam," I said deliberately. "I realize you have not been part of our household for long, and it might be that you did not realize you *were* now part of our household. But this," I gestured to the facts before us, "is not something Marius does lightly. Not in our house. You are Ashvi's brother, my intellectual guide, and – I trust – my friend. If Marius has not yet told you our history, I expect it is only a matter of time. Let me assure you I am truly, wholly, *unspeakably* delighted that he has found someone to care for. He deserves it. As, I'm sure, do you. As do I," I added. "But I have rather more opportunities for such frolics than either of you might. Donald, for instance." Sunnam made a shocked sound.

"You're shameless, Lizzie." Marius' tone was so affectionate.

I patted him again, letting my fingers trail up to his muscular thigh. Those curly hairs, mmm, how my skin loved the feel of them. I told myself to stop it; he was otherwise engaged tonight; regretfully withdrew my hand and placed it decorously in my lap. I could use it for other purposes later. "To answer your question, I did learn a few useful things. Another guest tonight was a man recently come from Ceylon. He told a fascinating story about his great-grandfather, banished there by his noble English family, who discovered on their property a vein of fine gemstones. He is unmarried and I suppose he's come to England for that purpose, though he didn't say so. Possibly because I was the only other unmarried guest." I shrugged. Mr. LaSalle was a fine-looking man, but marriage was not for me. As I believed I'd made clear. "I asked about the mining operation after dinner, which happily caused the gossipy wives to flee my vicinity. And I came away with a list of books to order." I dug in my bodice for the crumpled paper, squinted at the scribbled list, and handed it to Sunnam. "Legible enough?"

He smoothed the paper, studied it for a moment, then set it aside. "Sufficiently. From Ceylon, you say?"

Ah, excellent, his mental function was restored. "Yes, and I had some hard questions for him about his native workers, but he stood up to them quite well. His ancestor married a native woman and he considers many of the workers his family. Needless to say, he's a scandal and an outrage to other property holders in the colony, but he doesn't seem to take that to heart." And Fairchild had met him in London, but that was neither here nor there. I organized my limbs and removed my person from the bed, stooping to pick up my shoes. "I will leave you in peace now. Sunnam, let me assure you that while Marius is free to visit you in your rooms, you are always welcome here. For dinner, or breakfast, or the in-between." I gave them both a nod and a smile, then left them alone. Once he took his degree I hoped he might consider living with us permanently, but that was an invitation for Marius to make. This might not be the love that would fill the Toby-shaped hole in my friend's heart. On the other hand, it might.

The door to my bedchamber was ajar; I could see the glow of a fire. Stepping in, I looked around for Daisy; she came through from the dressing room. "You didn't have to wait up."

"It's not late. And I thought you might want a bit of company."

"Since our Marius is otherwise engaged?" She laughed. I rolled my eyes. "You know you are never second choice."

"Dear Miss Lizzie. I'm well aware you need variety. As it happens, I'm in the mood tonight." She was behind me, beginning on my buttons.

"Did you have dinner with them? Did Ashvi join you? How long did Sunnam take to relax?"

"Yes, yes, and he never did." She started telling me about it while we got me out of my clothes – I do love clothes, but they are so *complicated* – and into a new cashmere nightdress. Then the jewelry was put away, and my complicated coiffure deconstructed. Finally we sat by the fire together, sipping Ashvi's mint tea, talking about our next adventure. I hoped to see Fairchild when she returned from London. Until then, I saw no reason not to make myself free of England. I'd barely left Oxford since arriving; the worst of the settling-in was accomplished; the household could undoubtedly do without me for a while. Everyone could do with some time off, in other words, and they wouldn't take it while I was in residence.

"I met a man at dinner whose family is based in Yorkshire," I said, leaning my head on the high back of my chair, smiling at Daisy. She always looks her best by firelight. Tonight she was wearing her favorite calico slip under my favorite velvet dressing gown. "I thought you and I might take the train up to York. You look so pretty tonight."

"So do you," she said, smiling, no doubt at how distractible I was. Setting her cup down on the little marquetry table between us, leaning across it. I met her halfway for a kiss.

Some time later, when we were comfortably resting in bed, I returned to the subject of escaping Oxford. "Shall I send Marius to the Equatorial Club to inquire after a lodging in York? Once we know there's a suitable place, I can have Donald send a wire to reserve us rooms." Arriving in a strange city without confirmed plans was a guarantee of discomfort, especially since few establishments that met my standards also welcomed persons of color as guests. And under no circumstances would I send Daisy to stay in some dockside tavern while I reposed myself in a whites-only hotel.

As to the wire: of course I was perfectly capable of composing a telegram myself, but (first) any commercial establishment tended to treat a solicitor's correspondence more seriously than that of an untitled woman, and (second) it was the sort of small favor which Donald particularly appreciated doing for me. Men do like to feel needed.

Daisy lifted her head from my shoulder, gazed at me for a moment, then laid it down again. "I'll go myself. Haven't been to the club for ages."

"I've kept you all too busy."

"Suppose you think the others will be idle while you're away."

"While *we're* away. I hope so. We've wrought some great changes in a short time. If I'm ready for a proper holiday, surely everyone else is too. Heaven knows I've done less of the actual work than any of you."

"You are not so very much trouble." She sounded amused. I shifted enough to kiss her forehead, then settled back. How did other unmarried women of my sort manage? I despised sleeping alone. Had never even known that about myself before Daisy. So many things I didn't know, I thought drowsily. No doubt I was smiling as I fell asleep.

Fairchild

Dinner at Sybil's was more enjoyable than expected, which meant I'd sequestered myself far too long. Even a person such as myself, comfortable in silent solitude, can benefit from regular applications of society. The colonial turned out to be an older gentleman (by which I mean at least ten years older than myself) possessed of property in Ceylon; master of a century-old gem mine there; and cousin, of some degree, to the current Marquess of Rowland. He was cultured, handsome, prosperous, and charming; no wonder the ladies of London were all a-flutter. I indicated that he was welcome to call upon me should he find himself in Oxford or its environs, and privately thought Miss Bonner would greatly enjoy meeting him.

As might Inigo. Something about the man told me he was not in the market for a wife.

Over the next week, I re-acquainted myself with various more-or-less close friends; did some more essential (according to Polly) shopping; lifted a pint with my friend at the Yard; went to the theatre with Amelia; and quite easily traced Agatha Fletcher, née Cavill, to lodgings not far from the Boudica. Having determined that she clerked for an importer and generally returned home no earlier than eight o'clock, I sent in my card indicating I'd call the following evening. If we got on, I'd invite her to dine at the club on another day. My inquiries did not prepare me for the reality of her.

Shown up to her rooms, I was met by a person nearly my own height, sturdily built, and only nominally female. She wore her hair as short as mine; it was medium-brown, dusted with gray. No cosmetics to enhance a sallow complexion, bearing the faint lines and softened edges of four decades. Below the epicene countenance was a worn but tidy brown suit, by which I mean trousers, vest, and jacket. She studied me for a moment, no doubt making similar observations. I was dressed almost the same. "George Fairchild, I presume," she said, and stood back.

I inclined my head and stepped into the room. My first observation was of genteel poverty, which came as no surprise. My second, which *was* a surprise, was the woman reclining on a chaise. She wore a loose gray woolen gown, with a plaid wrapped around her shoulders and a molting fur rug over her legs. "I beg your pardon," I said.

"You're most welcome, your grace," she said without moving.

"My friend Catriona," Agatha said. "Come and sit. Why've you sought me out?" She pulled a chair closer to her presumably-ill friend (probably lover) and indicated another.

Not shy, was she? Barely civil. Well, she'd no cause to care much for Society or its judgements. I lifted the second chair, so as not to drag it across the threadbare carpet, and brought it closer to my host. We were all now grouped around the fireplace, in which reposed a miserly heap of glowing coals. "I heard of an altercation in Belgravia and came to see if I could help."

They both stared at me, then at each other. After a moment Agatha cleared her throat and said, cautiously, "Help?"

"If your brother has in some way withheld or otherwise done you out of your inheritance, as I've come to believe based on some discreet inquiries, I may have the resources to influence your case."

Another silence, another unspoken exchange. "Don't you want to know why I live this way?"

"My dear, it couldn't matter less to me. As you can see, conventionality is not my chief concern."

A stifled laugh from Catriona, which became a muffled cough. I gave her a concerned glance; she shook her head. "Not consumption," she said in a thready voice. "But the London air."

Agatha took the woman's hand. "They call it weak lungs. Last winter she had pneumonia. I want to take her away, to the South, for sunshine and fresh air. That bastard Leighton holds a small bequest from my uncle which would, I believe, secure us a modest living."

My mind was already racing. I happened to know of a farm in Provence where two women could live, at ease in the sun, in perfect comfort. The owners considered themselves in my debt, or rather Freddy's, which amounted to the same thing. "This bequest, is it an investment, or an object?"

"Both, in fact. Two thousand pounds and an artifact from South America."

"Tell me more." And oh, the tale she spun me, of her adventurous uncle who brought back a bejeweled golden collar from the Amazon. She produced a bundle of letters; selected and unfolded one; the author described the thing and promised it, along with the stated funds, to 'my dear niece, daughter of my heart.' I handed the letter back; she returned it to its place like the treasure it undoubtedly was. "Your husband didn't try for it?"

"I never told him about it. Fifteen years ago, my uncle was still alive. After certain events, when my bloody thief of a brother showed me the door," she shrugged. "It took years to scrape together the funds for a solicitor. Then I'd met Catriona, and we took lodgings together."

"Illustrator," the other woman said softly. "For a fashion house."

Ah. That accounted for the easel by the window, the paint-box, the jar of brushes. I might be able to put her in the way of additional work, if she wanted it. But first, to settle Sir Leighton Cavill's hash. "With your permission, I'll consult some friends. I've no doubt we can see you settled before Christmas. Mr. Fletcher," I said quite deliberately, "would you care to dine with me at the Boudica Club tomorrow night? We could discuss this in more detail. Quite privately, I assure you."

A worried look at Catriona. "Would you be all right, love?"

"For heaven's sake, Aggie."

The fond smile pinched at my heart. I took my leave shortly after. On arrival at the club, I made arrangements for several deliveries. Coal; a hamper of food; a pot of eucalyptus unguent from America that I'd found superbly effective in easing congestion of the lungs; a jar of high-quality lamp oil. I was never ashamed of my wealth, but when reminded of how very little (to me) money it took to provide such comforts, I cringed.

Sir Leighton Cavill, the bloody thief, was in some ways untouchable. But I'd have that artifact off him one way or another, and the two thousand pounds with it.

A week later I was back in Oxford, and the game was afoot. I told Inigo everything; he suggested consulting a solicitor of our acquaintance; and I rather incautiously mentioned the affair to Miss Bonner when she called on me upon her return from York.

"I won't breathe a word," she assured me, resting her hand on my arm for a moment. "But can I help? If this person's greedy enough to hold back his own sister's inheritance, he might be greedy enough to sell it."

I blinked at her. I'd been thinking along less obvious lines. "I'd a fancy to steal it," I admitted, and we both started cackling. "The things I say to you!" I wiped tears of laughter from my eyes. She was grinning; no other word for it. "Will you dine with me?"

"I'd be delighted," she said promptly. "But I rode here today."

"I can send you back in my carriage. Or," I ventured, "you're very welcome to stay the night." We stared at each other, the moment modulating in a way that raised the hairs on the back of my neck. Her lips were slightly parted, eyes warm; chin tipped up so I couldn't help but notice the white throat above her collar, and the tantalizing curve of bosom lower down. I had to remind myself to breathe.

"I'd be *delighted*," she said, "to stay the night."

The remainder of that day (and night) would become, I was positive, a cherished memory. We spent the afternoon talking about ourselves and our households. Elizabeth told me how she came to know her dresser Daisy, and her steward Marius; I told her about Freddy and Caroline. At first only the outlines, because we had so much to say. The details came later, after a dinner taken privately in my study.

"I brought Daisy out of another house on Fifth Avenue," she told me in the quiet dark, when we lay in my bed, her silky hair spread across my chest. "I'd been invited to dinner and caught the oldest son, the man I was supposed to be considering for marriage, molesting her in the hall. I slapped his face, because she couldn't, then told her she'd a place in my house for the asking. She went home with me and we've never been parted since."

"And Mr. Knight?"

"He was a childhood friend of Daisy's. She came across him one day when she was at liberty because I was suffering through afternoon tea with an aunt. He'd been injured at work, building the underground train. His partner was killed in the same accident. She brought him home and hid him in our kitchen. Of course the cook sent a message to me as soon as I was home, so I went down to meet him. I go to his bed sometimes," she whispered, very still.

I thought about this for a minute, then put two fingers to her chin, lifting her head to make eye contact. "What will you do if you find yourself with child?"

Oh, the relief in that beautiful smile. "A man who isn't willing to use a prophylactic is not a man I'm willing to use." I huffed out a laugh. She kissed my breast. "But if it happens, c'est la vie. My household can accommodate a child, and I suspect he'd love to have one. Everyone knows," she added. "All of us, we're conspirators. Me and Daisy, me and Marius, Marius and Sunnam. The others either care more for us than for convention, or they simply don't care."

"More often than you'd think, people don't." I kissed her forehead. "Meeting Freddy changed my life in every single way. I can't tell you how I'd dreaded the prospect of marriage. I knew I didn't desire men, barely suspected I desired women, but truly didn't grasp the possibilities until I knew Freddy well enough for him to introduce Inigo. Then," I made a grand gesture, as if the sun of comprehension now shone upon me. Elizabeth was giggling. "Our marriage was such a constant adventure, I didn't feel the lack of, well, this." Now I stroked from her hair down her back and patted her bottom. "Once he was gone, the entire family insisted I must have a companion, and I got on well enough with Caroline to make the suggestion. Then I put her to the test."

"Fairchild! You rake!"

We both laughed. "Not like that, you vixen. I wanted her to go with me on an expedition. Told her, you will live for days at a stretch in the same garments; you will never have a proper bath. Any water in which you may find yourself immersed will provide you close acquaintance with fish, leeches, and various carnivorous reptiles. You will eat a tedious diet of cured meat, porridge, and fruit. You will be too hot, too cold, filthy, exhausted, and infuriated a majority of the time. Are you certain this is something you wish to experience?"

Elizabeth said softly, "She must have said yes."

I sighed. "Else she had not been my companion for so long. Yes. She said, I have lived my whole life confined in various rather luxurious boxes. If physical discomfort is the price of freedom, I shall willingly pay it." I glanced over at Elizabeth. "I will confess that by the end of our trip I was more attentive to her comfort." She must have taken my meaning; she gurgled with laughter. I tsked. "Wicked girl."

She was so unlike me. Lushly feminine, soft and yielding, with the unabashed sensuality of a cat. The knowledge that she indulged her passions with others might disturb some; to me it was a relief. I was not the person who could be everything to another. Too much of myself was mine alone.

Perhaps as much to the point, our several conversations satisfied me that all parties were involved by mutual consent; free to engage, or not, as they chose. I gave Elizabeth to understand that her secrets were now my own, and that should any of her household require a confidential (if not wholly objective) ear, mine was available. By the next morning, we were assured that the things she wanted from me were precisely the things I could give.

Among those things: a solution to the case of the bloody thief, the product of a solid two hours' scheming over breakfast in my private study. Then followed a consultation with Inigo, after which I sent my laughing girl back to Oxford. "Au revoir," I promised as she mounted.

"Au revoir," she echoed, tapping her hat with her riding crop. Then she ran her gloved thumb under her bottom lip, smiled roguishly, and clicked to her horse. I watched her ride away, still on the step when she disappeared into the wood.

"What are the odds," I said later to Inigo, "that I should *thrice* meet a person who fills up the empty spaces in me?"

"Incalculably poor," he said, packing his pipe. He did not meet my eyes, and I instantly regretted my words. In the years since Freddy died, Inigo had not been wholly alone, I knew. But the occasional private encounter was not the same as sharing someone's life. I did not expect to live with Elizabeth; it would not be the same relationship I had with Caroline; but it would be more, perhaps, than Inigo might ever have again. He must have felt my gaze; he looked up, producing a half-smile, with half a shrug. "Your happiness is of value to me, Duchess."

"All the same. I'm sorry." A suggestion was on the tip of my tongue; if Agatha and Catriona could be relocated to Provence, perhaps Inigo would join them. The law was different there, and the weather closer to that of Spain. But I held my peace. The French solution was yet a mere possibility; better I say too little than too much. And there was the gentleman from Ceylon to consider. I happened to know he'd recently taken lodgings at the Equatorial; it was time to issue an invitation.

Elizabeth

The Desperate Venture upon which Fairchild and I embarked was, let me be plain, a mere Frolic. We could, with a discreet advertisement and a few weeks' gossip, secure the desired access. What remained was a matter of presentation. We took certain people into our confidence, enlisting their aid in certain ways, and let the bloody thief come to us.

I was wild to meet Agatha Fletcher and her friend, but that must wait until the acquisition was complete. If I were seen visiting them, or meeting with them, word might get back to Cavill and spike our guns. The best I could do was deploy new friends in London to find me some examples of Catriona's artwork.

Meanwhile I had, for the first time, a woman in my life whose mental faculties surpassed my own. Daisy, having met Fairchild's dresser Polly, was happy to continue warming my bed (in the literal sense) but now preferred to reserve more intimate activities to a different person. I thought this more than fair. Honestly, by the end of a given day's study I was more apt to retire with a soothing cup of Ashvi's bedtime tea than with a friend to help settle my mind. Between Fairchild (with whom I studied modern languages, socioeconomic geography, and political history, also fencing), Marius (with whom I met daily on matters of business), and Sunnam (with whom I read Greek, Latin, and literature), my mind was too fatigued to be unsettled. It was glorious.

Fairchild and I came to understand each other very well in very little time. We each reserved certain privacies; we each craved certain intimacies. We spoke to each other, within weeks, as lifelong friends. I both respected and envied the life she'd built with the Duke and Inigo; she respected and envied the life I had with

Marius et al. Not that she wished for one exactly like it: Fairchild required a good deal more solitude than I ever would.

But I had been primed to fall headlong into love with her, and she did nothing to discourage me. While we did not say so, I knew from the way she held and kissed me that she felt the same.

She was so very different from me. Her body, while yet a woman's, was firm and strong as a man's. We rode together, rambled, went punting. If I joined her for dinner after such exertions, I inevitably stayed the night. If she came to Oxford, somehow she rarely returned home before morning. We talked for hours, with and without the gentlemen of our acquaintance. It was the fullest friendship I could imagine, let alone wish for.

And along with that, I had my private enclave of select friends, the family of my heart. "Have you ever known the like?" I asked idly, one morning as Daisy and I consulted with Ashvi and Mary in the kitchen garden.

Ashvi frowned at me. "What, the garden?"

"No, I beg your pardon. I was thinking of our household."

Her face displayed comprehension. "Never the like," she said. "Only you would make such a home."

"Or someone like me," I suggested, which garnered a derisive snort from Daisy. "What?"

"If there *is* anyone else like you, which I doubt." She glanced at our bright-eyed housemaid. "What say you, Miss Mary?"

"I don't believe I know enough to have an opinion, Miss Daisy," quoth the girl.

To which I replied, “That never stopped me!”

Fairchild

Oh, that darling girl. I had, for the first time in my life, a woman friend whose mental faculties challenged my own. Elizabeth had not the deep need for physical activity that I’d discovered alongside Freddy; perhaps her physicality expressed itself in her intimate relationships. She was healthy, vigorous, and increasingly strong, but we both knew she did not crave extremities of exertion.

She was, let me be plain, a domesticated creature. I thought no less of her for that.

We saw each other almost daily. With very little open negotiation, we established our mutual limits. Our plan to secure the Emerald Boa felt something between a game and a military campaign, requiring all the shrewdness she’d employed to extract herself from New York and all the boldness I’d employed to seize the life Freddy offered me.

I would always regret that Caroline left me so soon. She’d been the companion I needed in those years, and I believe we would have remained friends for the entirety of both our lives. But this new friendship – call it what it was: this new love – served so much more of me. It was glorious.

Inevitably, as I looked ahead, my thoughts turned to adventure. Between my wedding trip and losing Caroline, I’d not gone a year without some lengthy absence from England. Before meeting Elizabeth, I’d desired nothing more than a berth on a steamer bound for points south. Now I found myself thinking: where could we go together.

There was so much of the world – most of it, in fact – that Elizabeth had yet to see. Her interests were infinite and her energy nearly so. But she was newly come both to Oxford and to independence; for me to lure her away so soon would be unkind.

I decided to topple Society's expectations and rejoin it for a while. England was not devoid of interesting people, but I'd seen few of them with any frequency in the past fourteen years. Once we disposed of Sir Leighton Cavill, I could reintroduce myself to the social whirl. With a few well-placed words, I could ensure that Elizabeth was welcomed everywhere. She'd already made friends in London. The thought of it was unexpectedly pleasant. It seemed, in fact, like a proper frolic.

When I put the question to her, she lit up like a Roman candle. "Ooh! Really?"

Could I do anything but smile? "I haven't accepted the Duke's invitation for Christmas since the year after Freddy died. He won't know what to do with himself. I'll warn you, his wife is full of social strictures."

She made a dismissive sound and cuddled against me. "I refuse to be daunted by strictures. Where do they live?"

"Surrey. Have you been there?"

"Never a minute. Will we go by train?"

This assumption, that we would travel together, pleased me. Naturally, I'd make my attendance contingent on hers. All the incumbent Duke and his family need know was that Elizabeth was my good friend. After years during which Caroline was always at my side for my occasional social appearances, no one would question that I had a new companion. "We will. They'll expect us each to come with a servant."

That led to a brief discussion of how best to ensure Daisy's comfort in a household where she might be the only person of color. Elizabeth took the question home, and returned to me with a counter-proposal. "Daisy says she'd rather not. A friend of hers from the Equatorial is going to York, and invited her along, and Daisy liked the city when we went. So if it suits, might I bring Mary instead?"

I of course agreed. Before long the arrangements were made. Once the word got out, more invitations arrived, in sufficient numbers that at least half my prospective hosts must be disappointed. "It's as you said," I told my dresser Polly after sending a few notes of regret. "They heard I said yes to someone and now they all want me."

"Must be exhausting to be in such demand," she said in a tone of desiccating dryness.

I meant to return something in kind, then remembered. "Do you mind that Daisy's off to York when we go to the Duke?"

"Good gracious, no. We'd hardly see each other there, and never in private. She'll have a holiday and then come home with stories to tell."

Stories: the currency of every social group. What a turn my own story had taken!

The thought recurred as I sat at table with new and old friends at Chez Bonheur. Elizabeth was not an egalitarian in the purest sense; she was neither blind to, nor dismissive of, social distinctions. She was, however, both free and able to suit herself in the privacy of her own home, as I was myself. The result was a dinner gathering including:

Myself, a dowager Duchess with antecedents recorded for centuries past;

Inigo, a Spaniard of noble birth whose family tree was as extensive as mine;

Donald Richards, a gentleman of modest family, the sort of man my social peers might employ or even meet at a pub, but not invite to dine;

Sunnam Gould, born in England to Colonial parents who, I was given to understand, had not come to our island entirely by choice;

Severin LaSalle, born in Ceylon of mixed parentage, a social favorite due to a combination of (if we speak plainly) his highly-ranked and wealthy connections, his personal charm, and my peers' avid curiosity;

Marius Knight, Elizabeth's steward, whose white father was unknown to him and whose black mother had been born a slave; and, of course:

Elizabeth herself. How she blossomed in company. Especially, it appeared, company that would have the social hens clucking: unequal numbers! No genteel lady companion! Such a *variety* of men! Such dashing style! Tonight she wore an evening gown of lavender silk, but with her hair informally dressed. The necklace she'd worn when we all went in to the dining room was now in LaSalle's hand.

He inspected it closely, eyes narrowed, then looked up. "One prefers sunlight," he said ruefully. "Was this a family piece?"

Elizabeth set down her glass, shaking her head. "Oh no. The ornaments passed down to me, aside from my mother's pearls, are of no account. I found this in London, specifically to accompany this dress." She gestured, then smiled. "And a few others in similar shades."

"You like purple," I murmured. "And it suits you."

"Thank you! So obliging." She gave me one of those looks, a private sort of look that, no doubt, fooled no one. Then, with a flutter of eyelashes, she returned her attention to LaSalle. "I was told the stones are topaz, but I simply don't believe it."

"Wise of you," he said, passing the necklace across the table. "I should rather say jade."

"Jade?! I thought jade was always green?"

"No, indeed. Most commonly so, but also to be found in white, yellow, pink, and," he tipped his head to indicate the jewels in question, "lavender. Such opacity is not to be found in gem-quality topaz, and while pink topaz was once a social favorite, I have never seen it occur in *that* color."

"Then my suspicions are justified," Elizabeth said happily, holding her hair up as Marius fastened the necklace for her. "How fortunate that I drove the price down. Oh, my dears, how I *haggled*."

All the men laughed, though LaSalle was shaking his head. "In the Orient, your jade is of greater value than topaz. You made a canny bargain."

This clearly pleased Elizabeth no end. "It's as well. Marius would tell you I've done nothing but spend money since arriving in England."

"That's what it's for," he murmured affectionately. "And you don't waste it."

"Some might disagree," she said. After a sip of wine, she tipped her head to indicate the library.

Donald, glass in hand, smiled around the table. "Very few here in Oxford would quarrel with your books."

I glanced at him doubtfully. "In a woman's hands?"

He winced. "Ah. Well, perhaps. But *I* say Miss Bonner sets a good example," he added stoutly. "There are as many women as men, and surely we cannot afford to disregard your mental powers." He raised his glass to me, then to Elizabeth.

"Are you then a suffragist?"

He met my challenge squarely. "I am."

I raised my glass to him in turn. "I will confess I was not, until I traveled out of England. But then," with a self-deprecating shrug, "I was young."

"Younger," he returned with another smile.

He meant I was still young, and in absolute terms I was. Inigo, mostly quiet for the past quarter-hour, was the eldest in this gathering. I looked down the table at him. "And you, amigo?"

"Young, no; a suffragist, yes." His smile was somehow distributed equally between me and LaSalle. "Like Mr. Richards, I believe a society is strongest when it welcomes and encourages all talents."

"And in that, I believe, we are all agreed." Elizabeth nudged Marius; he reached for the bottle on the table (how *very* informal) and poured some wine into her glass. A moment later we'd each received a top-up. He set down the empty bottle and we raised our glasses. Elizabeth said, "To talent!"

"And books!" Donald suggested.

"And money," Marius added. I laughed into my glass, barely avoiding a sputter, which made all the others laugh. Even quiet, diffident Sunnam. He met my gaze, glanced sideways at Marius, and produced an expression eloquent of 'these two.'

Elizabeth

The next few weeks were highly educational. Between my ongoing lessons with Sunnam, new lessons with Fairchild, and yet more lessons with Mr. LaSalle – who proved to be not at all interested in securing a wife – I could not have wished for more stimulation. And after a few words in the right ears, I had an appointment with Sir Leighton Cavill.

I suppose I ought to have felt nervous. This expedition was, while perfectly legal in intent, also deceptive in practice. But Fairchild said time was of the essence, and I believed her. I was no stranger to the speed with which a motivated individual could make off with someone else's property. It had not happened to me personally, but those stories were common in my former circle. Until the suit was settled – which might be years – Cavill would have no possible motivation to give Agatha her due, and every motivation to sell off or conceal what he could.

She said she had no proof that the necklace was intended for her, beyond that letter. It had been witnessed, but all the parties involved were long dead. The best we could do was get the damned thing off him before he thought to sell it. And the simplest way to do that was for me to give him the idea, and buy it myself.

Fairchild could have, of course. Except she was – well, not to say notorious, but certainly *known* – in short, not a person Cavill might be expected to do business with. He was squarely on the side of Women Should Be Seen And Not Heard. Women who were photographed in trousers at fencing clubs were an outrage beyond bearing. Especially when they had more money than he did.

That did not affect our intention of going in together. They had never met in person, and for him to recognize her from one of those indistinct photographs was unlikely. Especially since she would be in character as my fencing master. Cavill would, in any case, already be distracted by Marius, masquerading as my solicitor.

We alighted from the hired carriage ten minutes before the appointed time. Ceremoniously welcomed by a butler less imposing than Amon, ushered promptly up a grand staircase to a drawing-room, offered tea: all the courtesies. Well, the man knew I was a person of considerable means, if little breeding. I was dressed for the part. A flattering ensemble, if I did say so myself: crisp shirtwaist, long skirt and matching nip-waisted jacket of fine gray-violet tweed with a thread of yellow. Liberty silk cravat printed with yellow flowers on a field of violet. A dark-gray hat trimmed with silk violets; gray kid boots with two-inch heels that gave me such a swagger – oh, I did love this costume.

Marius wore one of Sunnam's suits. It fit him well, if not quite perfectly. His own best suit would have served, but this one had that indefinable quality which said 'made to order for someone who is not quite gentry.'

Fairchild, meanwhile … Great Scott. Suffice to say my first reaction was to swoon, and my second to giggle. Or maybe it was the other way around. She was done up in the most bohemian suit one can imagine, with a mustache made (so she told me) of her own hair. Each hair sewn to the finest net, the finished appliance (her word) affixed to her skin with spirit gum, the edges obscured with cosmetic. The urge to kiss her was Very

Strong, and no doubt obvious; she said, "Later," which made me giggle again.

"Miss Bonner."

I ceased my study of the little-used room (it had that dejected air, despite being perfectly clean and prettily furnished) and turned to face the door, setting my teacup aside. Rising to shake my host's hand. "Sir Leighton. Much obliged for your time today."

"Your solicitor's letter intrigued me." His glance passed over Marius as if he were not there, then sharply returned. "I understood he would be with you. Is this Mr. Knight? Or – "

I interrupted his half-turn toward Fairchild. "Indeed, this is Mr. Knight." I did not suggest that Marius should offer his hand, but gave him a look that meant 'a bow, if you please.' He clasped his hands behind his back and inclined his head gravely. "And this is my fencing master, Mr. Diaghilev."

Another sharp glance. "As in Les Ballets Russes?"

"My cousin." Fairchild said that with a pronounced Slavic accent, and an air of weary indulgence bespeaking years of answering that question. "How do you do." She offered a callused hand; Sir Leighton shook it; she stepped back. Good Lord, the way she moved; I cannot do it justice.

"I've brought Pyotr along to look at the blade," I explained. "The expert eye, you know." There: just enough to excuse bringing a third party.

"This is, ah, for your personal use, Miss Bonner?"

"Oh yes. I've only just begun to fence, but it is a most exhilarating exercise, don't you agree? Having my own blade is an indulgence." I produced a feminine half-shrug meant to convey that yes, I was a silly woman, and also that I could afford to indulge myself. "But we mustn't take up too much of your time."

The bloody thief was well-trained; he understood that I meant to relieve him of my dark-skinned and foreign companions, as well as my vaguely unladylike self, without delay. "Will you join me in my study, then?" He made a gesture encompassing the three of us, which was a bit of a relief. I wanted Marius with me, much as he might have preferred to be left in the drawing-room with the tea and biscuits.

We followed our host down a hall and into another room. This one was inhabited: the scent of pipe tobacco, a drinks table, faded rugs on the parquet floor and a floor cushion, redolent of dog, in a corner. One wall was taken up with shelves crowded with books – many popular editions, as well as older volumes in well-worn leather bindings – and interesting artifacts. Marius drifted toward that end of the room while Fairchild and I joined Sir Leighton at his desk. A gleaming saber lay atop it, in an open case. I did not have to pretend enthusiasm. I peppered him with questions; he answered them; I bashfully asked if I might hold it; he courteously lifted it from the case and offered the hilt to me.

Thanking all the gods (as Fairchild would say) that I had taken well to fencing, I essayed a few movements in the open center of the room. It was, in all honesty, a lovely weapon. Light, flexible, well-balanced. "Dear sir," I said after a few minutes. "How on earth can you bear to part with it?"

He coughed out a laugh. "My son doesn't care for fencing, my dear, and I've not done any for decades. This was bought for me as a practice blade; it is not a family heirloom. When your inquiry reached me, I was intrigued. And now I should be happy to see it go with you."

In other words: a few hundred pounds for a sword taken not from a Frenchman at Waterloo but from a commercial traveler in Salzburg will be useful just now. "Oh! I *am* delighted! You are *so* kind!" I caught a quelling look from Fairchild that told me I was overdoing it. "Well, there is certainly no need for me to go on to the next prospect, is there, Pyotr?"

She silently held out her hand; I gave her the hilt; she performed a stunning demonstration ending with a twist of her wrist that described a flashing circle with the blade. "It is adequate," she said grudgingly, laying it back in the case.

I nearly laughed. "Excellent. We will send a telegram from the station so as not to waste Lord – ahem, anyone's time." Oh, Cavill liked that. "And now we have most of the afternoon ahead of us. It's always so pleasant to find extra time, isn't it, Sir Leighton?"

"It is indeed."

I gave him an approving smile and said, "This is your private study, is it not, sir? These things all seem quite personal." I was moving toward the shelves, because I had not missed Marius' sideways nod. "Mr. Knight, perhaps you could prepare the draft for Sir Leighton?"

"Of course, miss." Raising his eyebrows in inquiry, he gestured to one of the leather-covered chairs in the corner, with a small table alongside; our host made a 'yes of course' gesture in return. Marius drew my check-book and a fountain pen from his inside pocket and took a seat. I knew he would make a show of writing out the draft. "And the amount?"

I made a show of being flustered. "Oh, good heavens. I seem to recall your secretary suggested three hundred pounds, sir. Is that satisfactory?" His secretary had in fact suggested two hundred fifty, which the man surely knew, but he did not contradict me. "Three hundred, Mr. Knight," I told Marius, turning my back to Sir Leighton for a moment so he wouldn't see my crossed eyes.

Marius choked back a laugh. "Yes, miss."

I returned my attention to the shelf in question. "Great Scott!"

"What is it?" As intended, Sir Leighton crossed the room to join me.

I had the leather-bound box open. The contents gleamed dully. It was crude. Barbaric. Some might say hideous. I *lusted* after it. "What on earth?" My voice was faint.

"Oh, I'd quite forgot that was here." Liar. "My uncle brought it back from South America years ago. He said it was called The Emerald Boa, but I don't see it. Not even sure those are emeralds."

Only an expert would be sure. To someone brought up on the sort of jewelry a titled woman was meant to wear – quite like the sort that I was accustomed to wearing; a society woman is considered not quite fully dressed without jewels, after all – the necklace was unprepossessing in the extreme. The stones were unevenly shaped, unevenly colored, unevenly sized; polished, not cut. They were laid out on thin plaques of gold, held in place with tabs of metal. One required some imagination to see a serpent in the overall composition; it was the central stone that lent any verisimilitude. The shape of a toy kite, with a broad ‘forehead’ having two distinct lumps, narrowing to a ‘nose;’ one might say this was the serpent’s head.

I was acutely aware that Fairchild had taken a seat near Marius, affecting complete disinterest in the proceedings. I gave Sir Leighton a doubtful look. “I can’t imagine anyone wearing that.”

“My wife said she wouldn’t have it in her rooms,” he said fondly. “And my daughter-in-law said it was only fit for amateur theatricals.” He looked at it with a sort of covetous pleasure that made my skin crawl. But what an opening he’d given me.

“Oh! Of course!” The fresh enthusiasm in my tone brought his attention back to me. I laid a hand on his forearm for a second. “I’ve been invited to a costume ball and none of my London friends have been the remotest help. They’ve suggested I should go as a red Indian, if you please. Or a Follies girl.” I widened my eyes at him and he produced an indulgent chuckle. “I could build a costume around this. If the ladies of your house don’t care for it, might I have it? Since I’ve got my check-book with me,” I added artlessly. “I’m sure that must be real gold, even if those are not real emeralds.” For a moment I held my breath, mind racing. If what he most wanted was to keep this from Agatha, selling it to me was (so far as he knew) the best possible way. A private sale was the only way he could shift it without exposing himself, after all. To place it with a reputable jeweler – the only sort who could verify its value – would require provenance, which he could not produce. He was already at law with Agatha, and he knew she had that letter. Far better to sell it to this silly impulsive woman, lie about when it was sold (if the question ever arose), and profit.

“There are few relics of my uncle’s travels,” he demurred after a moment.

I heard 'make it worth my while' and touched his arm again. "He had no children?" Because if he did, then this should have gone to them. Of course, thanks to Fairchild, I already knew the answer was No. Sir Leighton shook his head sadly. *What* a liar, pretending he wished there were another answer. Now I had to make an offer. He'd already said those might not be real emeralds, but we both knew they might indeed be. The thing came from South America, after all, and looked to have been made there. The amount of gold was trifling, worth a good deal less than the saber. If the stones were of the quality for fine jewelry – which they might well be, but only if cut, and by the time they were cut more than half the weight would be waste – the bulk of them might be worth … "Could I offer you a thousand pounds?"

He blinked. That was well under the possible value. But he had no right to sell it at all. I could *see* him thinking. He would make some reference to family history. "Most generous of you, Miss Bonner, but someday one of my grandchildren might like to have this."

"In twenty years the world will change again," I pointed out. "Your grandchildren might rather have an extra thousand pounds."

"Three."

I raised my eyebrows, concealing my triumph behind a calculating look. "How many grandchildren have you?" As if I didn't know.

The bloody thief almost laughed. "None, as yet."

"Two, then. Two thousand pounds. I shall be the talk of the costume ball. And I won't tell a soul where I got it," I assured him. "I'll make up a ridiculous story about rafting down the Amazon."

He was about to say Yes. "This costume ball of yours."

"It's in Paris," I invented. "An arts ball. Shockingly bohemian."

That did the trick. Now he knew none of his society friends would be there, or if they were they would never connect the outlandish American and her barbaric necklace with the Cavill who went to Colombia. "Done," he said. "Two thousand pounds. And you may take the case."

"Thank you, sir," I said most graciously, offering my hand. The blighter actually kissed it. The temptation to slap him was Very Strong. Instead I withdrew my hand in a lingering sort of way, as if I liked him holding it. "Another draft, Mr. Knight, if you would." I reached for the case, looked at the necklace once more, shuddered theatrically. "It's *so* awful!" Carried it to Fairchild. "Pyotr, may I trouble you? Thank you." She took the case with an air of disinterest. I noticed the saber case on the floor beside her chair. Marius finished writing out the second draft and handed the check-book and fountain pen to me. I took it from him with thanks, inspected the drafts, signed them with a flourish, and handed them to our host. "This has been a most diverting afternoon, Sir Leighton. Now I must be off to send that telegram so that Lord – ahem, no one expects me. Please give my regards to your family and tell them I shall wield your saber with honor."

"I'm sure you will, Miss Bonner. Let me walk you out."

Five minutes later, our carriage doors were closed and we were on our way. None of us said a word until we'd reached the railway station and disposed of the driver. “Well,” Marius said then, watching as the carriage joined the queue for new passengers, “back to Oxford? Or London?”

“London,” Fairchild said. “You’ll want to present your trophy to our friend.” She gave me a sidelong look.

“I mean to have it,” I said frankly. “But we must see her. Yes: London it is.” Marius, who was now holding the jewel case, handed it to me and went to see about our tickets.

“You were quite, quite brilliant,” Fairchild said softly. “I’ve known celebrated actresses who could not have carried that off so well.”

I blushed. “Oh! Do you think so? How lovely!” How lovely to be such an accomplished liar, so effectively deceitful, such a *bounder*. Her chin was tucked, shoulders shaking, free hand up to cover her mouth. The casual observer might think she was coughing. I dearly wished we were already safely behind a door at her club, so I could kiss that laughing mouth. With and without the mustache.

Fairchild

Elizabeth and I stayed at the Boudica long enough to see the thread wound up. My men at law consulted with Agatha’s; Sir Leighton’s advisors were counseled that she now held the Emerald Boa along with witnessed statements that he’d sold it, in clear contravention of his uncle’s wishes. A suggestion was made that the proceeds of that sale should be tendered to Agatha along with the sum promised her, in which case her suit would be withdrawn. Should the funds *not* be so tendered, the facts of the matter might regrettably become public.

Needless to say, we were all gratified, though not astonished, to hear that the bloody thief yielded. I then consulted a dealer well-qualified to assess the Emerald Boa. Elizabeth wrote another check. Finally, I consulted with Agatha and sent a wire to Provence.

A few weeks later I sat in the train compartment with Elizabeth, watching the French countryside roll by. I will confess to deep, not to say smug, satisfaction. Agatha and Catriona were in the next compartment, dizzily excited by the change in their circumstances. "I was afraid they might be too proud," I told Elizabeth, keeping my voice down.

"Had you been a man, possibly so."

It was a good point. Somehow aid from our sisters was so much easier to bear. "Was it a good adventure?"

"Oh, Fairchild, it was splendid! I know it's nothing like trekking the Andes or the Himalaya."

Those were things she knew I wanted. I gazed at her with concern, because much as I craved her company, she was not built for that sort of exertion. "If I go." Couldn't quite manage the rest: without you.

She gazed at me, hands clasped tightly in her lap. "I want the Pyramids. The Hagia Sophia. The Alhambra. The Taj Mahal. All of that with you, if I possibly may. And if you long for adventures that are beyond me, as at some point you surely will, let those be the times I stay behind to fill my brain. In Oxford, or at the foot of the mountains to wait for you. But do let us travel together. Three cabins, if you like; one for me, one for you, one for – oh, perhaps Mary? She could see to our needs splendidly. Plus she aspires to journalism, and a travel memoir could make her name for her. What do you say?"

I looked at her, glad there was no reason to disguise my fondness. "Four cabins, dearest. I may enjoy challenging my strength, but not by hauling my own trunks. We'll want a strong man to ensure your comfort."

She took that as I meant it. "Done. Marius flatly refuses another ocean crossing, but perhaps he may be persuaded to a coastal route. And of course I'll need Sunnam."

Meaning, Marius would need Sunnam. I stifled my laughter. Leaned across to kiss her. "Of course you will," I agreed.

THE END

Of

The Emerald Boa

Read on for

THE BLUE DRAGON

Donald

I stared – perhaps I *glared* – at the remarkable female I was honored to call my friend, and for the first time in my life understood the appeal of homicide. "I never thought you, of all people, would quote Jane Austen at me."

She bit her lip prettily, shrugged prettily, fluttered her eyelashes prettily. "Cheer up, Donald! You're a gentleman of means now! Thus I'm afraid that you really must marry. To attempt the management of a country estate on your own is a recipe for madness."

I threw myself onto one of her comfortable chairs, crossed one leg over the other, crossed my arms tightly over my chest, and sulked. "I am wholly unqualified to manage a country estate, no matter how many wives I might acquire. I've only ever lived in lodgings. Never had so much as a valet."

"And now you'll have a houseful of servants." She said it in a provoking 'there, there' tone of voice. "For heaven's sake. You're an intelligent man and you know dozens if not hundreds of useful people. If I could manage a move to a new country on my own, you can bloody well move to Leicestershire."

"It's pronounced *Lestershur*," I said moodily, as if correcting my favorite American would somehow confer mastery of this conversation. Then I sighed, unwound myself, and relaxed in an unmannerly sprawl because I knew she wouldn't mind. Gazed at her affectionately. "There's no point asking you, I suppose."

"None at all," she answered promptly, though with equivalent affection. "The last thing I want is to be married. I'll miss you, though." Slightly wicked tone there, the wicked girl. "I doubt your wife would care to share. I could write you a reference if you like?"

"Lizzie!"

She laughed, the shameless strumpet. "You should place an advertisement."

"A what?!"

"An advertisement," she said patiently. "I've seen plenty. Professional gentleman newly possessed of country estate seeks accomplished wife. Must play chess. Familiarity with horses a plus."

I stared at her again. "Why horses?"

"How do you think people navigate the countryside, you ninny? Traverse their estates? Pay calls hither and yon?"

That is not an invention: she did say 'hither and yon.' She was *mocking* me. If I had not been genuinely at a loss how to proceed, I should have gathered myself up and flounced out. Instead I thought about it. "She could be a widow," I suggested.

"A governess, perhaps?"

"Or a schoolmistress?"

"Someone intelligent," Elizabeth agreed. "With a sense of humor. You're giving up more than you know, taking this on. Leaving Oxford and all your friends, everything familiar."

"It's no great distance."

My objection was waved off with the authority of one who'd put an ocean between herself and her youth. "You've lived in this city all your life. What you want is someone who'll truly be a companion, not merely someone to keep house for you."

"Not too young," I mused.

"Though if you want children, not too old."

I blinked. Another thing I hadn't thought of. Did I want children? Marriage itself had seemed beyond my reach, but things were different now. A country house would have room for children. Room for them to play outdoors, on green grass, instead of in cobbled alleys as I had. "Someone who's lived in the country. Someone who likes it and won't constantly whinge about missing the city. Oh, Lizzie." I almost blushed at how breathy that sounded. As if I were exhaling years of limitations.

She came around behind my chair and leaned down, draping her arms over my shoulders and kissing my cheek. "You see? This is a *good* thing. If we're lucky, we can find you someone who'll tolerate me and the rest of your bohemian friends."

And so it began. Messages were sent, a conference was organized, and over the course of a long and wine-soaked dinner we wrote the advertisement. 'We,' you understand, being myself, Elizabeth, her good friend Fairchild, her steward Marius, his good friend Sunnam, and Sunnam's sister Ashvi, who ran Elizabeth's house like the tightest possible ship. When I read out the final version of the advertisement I looked at Ashvi with what might have been regret; I'd always quite fancied her; but she shook her head. Ah well. Upping sticks to the country was one level of discomfort for me, another entirely for her. We would simply have to see what kind of response this epic produced.

It was decided that Sunnam would conduct the interviews, in Elizabeth's library, for his convenience (he lodged with her now) and for hers (since she would undoubtedly pry into every stage of this endeavor). His nature and hers would prove a test for any applicant. While I wanted an intelligent, good-humored, capable wife, I also wanted a free-thinking one. I could, I believed, honestly swear to be true to a good woman; I would not conduct illicit affairs (much as it pained me to swear off my occasional frolics with Elizabeth); but I wouldn't care to treat my friendships as illicit. My friends, of all colors and creeds, must be welcome in my home.

Once the advertisement was placed, I packed my carpetbag and arranged my travel. It was time to see my new house. When I returned to Oxford, if the gods smiled upon me, I would have at least one potential wife to meet. I might be a *married* gentleman of means by midsummer 1906.

Till then, I should accustom myself to a new vision of the future. In the years since leaving university and launching my small practice, I'd traveled the length and breadth of England. One goes where the client's needs dictate, and thanks to the railway nearly all of the kingdom was accessible. I'd professional acquaintances from Scotland to Cornwall, people I could call friends in several fine cities, and a seldom-expressed appreciation for nature. The occasional holiday in wilder territory had met that need up to now. What would it be like to rise to a view of trees? To walk, every day, through woods or fields that belonged to me?

Before Elizabeth, I didn't truly know what I was missing. Breakfasting in her parlor, looking out on the river north of Oxford, hearing birds other than pigeons: luxury. Then there was the Duchess, on whose terrace I'd dined several times, again thanks to Elizabeth.

For years I'd made the best of a solitary, if not lonely, life. Each day was a circuit from my rooms to my office to one of several pubs. When the executor's letter found me, I had not yet begun to panic at my prospects, or to dread what might come if nothing changed. And now everything would change.

Aurelia

"Bollocking hell and bum." I threw the newspaper at the faded wallpaper beside the unlit fireplace. Another day without a hope of work. My most recent student (I use the term loosely) was making her debut this spring, and my services had been dispensed with. Instead of a governess, she would have a well-connected chaperone. She'd at least been sad to see me go, and had pressed a gift into my hands as I left the house. I had sufficient funds to see me through the year, if necessary, but I loathed being idle. I didn't like lodgings, with the commotion of other tenants all around me. And I was, after only a few weeks, already tired of London. So much noise. Filthy air. Filthy *everything*; if you've never tried to keep your linen clean in a rented room, you may count your blessings.

I lay back in my uncomfortable chair, staring at the dingy ceiling, wondering if there was any point going out. I'd no immediate need. Yesterday's visit to my agency had produced no leads; tomorrow, or the next day, would do. On my table were bread, cheese, a few apples; a spirit lamp, to heat my teakettle; my repeatedly-attempted, repeatedly-abandoned, second-hand copy of Don Quixote to read if I got truly desperate.

When I am not out of temper, I concede that London is a wonderful city. Even then I would apply the caveat: if you have money to spare. I could spend hours at the British Museum, and sometimes I did, when time and my purse permitted. My current residence was chosen for two factors, neither of which was proximity to the museum. The first was its availability for a weekly rent that I could manage, and the second was proximity to something else, namely the Boudica Club. I wasn't a member myself, but an old school friend of mine was. She lived in London year-round, so I'd shamelessly left a card once I came back to town. It went without saying that I wouldn't dine with her family, but we'd dined at the club several times. There was no point feeling mortified. Her family had money, mine didn't; she'd married a minor aristocrat, I worked for my living. I was not her social equal, and usually I didn't care. I am not the woman who will launch tumbrils over the fact that someone else can afford to give me a fine dinner in a warm room.

Was there anything at all worth reading in that newspaper? I ought to see. At the very least, reading it front to back would keep me away from Quixote a while longer.

Toward the back, I sat up abruptly. "What the devil." I shook the page, squinted at it, then lurched out of the chair and over to the window for better light. I had known, in a vague way, that newspapers contained personal advertisements that went beyond offers of work or of labor. I even knew that people sought personal connections (marital and otherwise) through the papers. Yet this particular missive astounded me. Possibly because so many words and phrases spoke to the things I'd given up hoping for.

> Gentleman Seeking Wife
>
> A solicitor currently of Oxford, coming into possession of a modest estate in Leicestershire, never before married, seeks helpmeet, companion, friend, and partner. Must play chess. Familiarity with horses a plus; also love of books, art, and the music hall. Age 25-35. Widows welcome to enquire. Our friends will be

academics, professionals, and adventurers of many nations. Write to Box 4A, the Equatorial Club, Oxford.

Must play chess! With that alone, the man severely limited his options. 'Of many nations' surely meant that at least one friend, if not the man himself, was a colonial. He didn't want a wife who would turn up her nose at someone from India, or Shanghai, or Gibraltar. I wondered if being bilingual was desirable. He very likely was himself.

The paper trembled in my hands. I hadn't been so excited since a particular handsome young officer escorted me to the opera. How long had this advertisement run? What if I'd already missed my chance? I had to write in response, immediately. Marriage had seemed beyond my reach for years. I knew, as perhaps this Oxford solicitor did not, what a hellish slog country life could be. But I'd had worse jobs.

I took a deep breath, set down the newspaper, and went to fetch my letter-box.

Dear Oxford Gentleman,

I am a thirty-year-old spinster currently at liberty, having worked since age eighteen as a lady's companion and governess. Educated at the Brighton Academy for Girls. My most recent employer is Sir Rupert G --. References available upon request. I play chess; speak three languages; was once an adequate rider; and adore the music hall. My father is a country vicar and my brother was called to the Bar three years ago.

Hoping for an opportunity to speak with you on these and other subjects, I am, most sincerely,

Aurelia Dashwood

Having revised the thing to the point of illegibility, I made a fair copy and ran down to post it. I spent the next three days pretending to look for a new position while actually waiting for a reply. The knock came at a low moment: I was about to give in to Quixote. Reprieved, I leaped to open the door; heard "Letter for you;" produced incoherent thanks and tuppence for the housemaid's trouble; then shut myself in again. Carefully opened the missive, with trembling hands. You may ask yourself why I should be so emotionally engaged by the prospect of matrimony with a complete stranger. Well, if you have never stared glumly into a future of constant insecurity looking after other people's children, you may count your blessings. I hoped rather intensely that this letter would not report the position already filled.

Dear Miss Dashwood,

Thank you for your letter. Please wire us a convenient day to appear in Oxford for an interview. We will reimburse your ticket.

Interview to be held by the undersigned at the home of Miss Elizabeth Bonner, appropriately chaperoned. Should our client's situation, as described in more detail, coincide with your interests, we will arrange a further meeting.

Sincerely yours,

Sunnam Gould, D. Phil.

The blighter wasn't even going to meet me himself? How offended should I be? But then, if he were, as implied, recently come to an unexpected legacy, he might fear encroaching fortune-hunters more than he feared giving offense.

This Gould must be one of the friends, most likely of Indian extraction. If he was insufferable, the solicitor probably was too. And vice-versa, of course.

I gave myself a day for research. Having been furnished the name, it seemed reasonable to conclude that Miss Bonner might appear in certain public records, which proved to be the case. The society pages in last year's papers connected her to the dowager Duchess of --, as well as to a fashionable favorite related to the Marquess of Rowland. She was not, in short, a person whose home I should hesitate to enter. Thus resolved, I sent the requested wire. I then stared discontentedly at the state of my wardrobe.

A lady's maid is one of the best-dressed servants in a society household; a governess, one of the worst. We must clothe ourselves according to our means. Mine had never been desperately pinched, but I was aware of every shilling. Over the past twelve years I'd served in four households, and only at Sir Rupert's had I leisure and funds sufficient to purchase new garments. On the one hand, my two-year-old gray dress, in the modern style with skirt and jacket, was perfectly appropriate for an interview. On the other hand, it was the best thing I owned. Which meant if I were to meet the Oxford Gentleman himself at some point, I must either wear the same blasted thing, or I must expect to buy new.

'New,' let it be said, meant 'lightly-worn second-hand.' I was not the woman to splash out for a bespoke dress. I had a neat enough figure and was not uncommonly tall; finding something in Petticoat Lane and having it tailored was the best solution. And perhaps I'd do that now, while I had the time. If the first interview went well, I'd want a new dress for the second. If it didn't, I'd want it anyway, for my next position. In the best-case scenario, I'd want an evening dress. I think I may be forgiven a frisson of excitement at the prospect.

> Dear Mum,
>
> I've decided to treat myself to a new dress or two. You'll say that's overdue, and you may be right. I plan to come home for a visit before the end of summer; shall I bring you anything?
>
> Recently saw a play called Major Barbara, the message of which I disagree with wholeheartedly. We shall argue about it with Father soon.
>
> Your loving daughter.
>
> p.s. the play is not yet published. Suffice to say it subscribes to the theory that financial assistance to the poor serves only to encourage them to remain poor. As you know, my theory is somewhat different.
>
> p.p.s. there is also an offensively stupid plot device concerning terms of inheritance.
>
> p.p.p.s. my tolerance for the assumption that a woman's moral compass is situational has never been lower.

My mother's reply came before I was quite finished securing the new additions to my wardrobe, which meant I was able to dispatch several related errands on her behalf as well as my own. I am not, I believe, a frivolous woman. But consider: I had been wearing the same two dinner dresses, with a series of repairs, alterations, and amendments, for nearly ten years. A well-made garment can be made to last a very long time when one is called upon to wear it no more than a few times per year.

Thus I make no apology for the sheer delight with which I approached the midsummer of 1906. Even if, by the end of it, I were to proceed not into marriage but into another post, at least I should do so better-clothed.

Donald

Oxford to Leicester is not a straight line. However, it is (as I'd told Elizabeth) no great distance. My new property was at the bottom of the shire, past the signpost for Rugby and before that for Lutterworth. The coach driver had no difficulty finding it; the area was little populated. As we approached I leaned so far forward to the window, I was practically on my knees. The drive was fairly smooth and graveled; the trees alongside it free of deadwood. A curve to the left, one to the right, and another left. We drew up before the house. It stood in a green park with a wood beyond; a dozen black-faced sheep grazed in front. The driver let down the steps and I climbed out. The crunch of wheels on gravel must have alerted the house; the front door swung open and a young man stepped out. "Mr. Richards?"

"So I am," I said, approaching. Climbed the steps and offered a hand, which he blinked at with surprise before gingerly accepting.

We shook, he let go, he stepped back. "I'm Morris," he said. "Henry. My mother's the housekeeper here."

"Mrs. Morris, of course." I followed him in, aware that the driver was speaking to someone behind me. Glanced over my shoulder to confirm that two more young men were seeing to my baggage. "How many are in the household?"

"The three you see, my mother, two maids, and a cook. I apologize for our informality, but there is no steward or bailiff."

"My dear man, I should hardly know what to say to one of those in any case. I did not expect this house to come to me. In fact, I didn't know it existed."

"Oh! No wonder, then."

"Mmm?"

"No wonder the old master never mentioned you."

I nearly laughed at that artless confession. There was a good chance that, had I not a circle of friends among men-at-law, the property could have reverted to the crown; the search for an heir had taken most of a year. My London friend Walpole had heard of it, seen the papers, and poked an astonished finger at them, saying "This puts me in mind of someone." Serendipity.

And my oath, it was an appealing house. Half-timbered, with a tidy slate roof, many chimneys, and whitewashed plaster. Morris walked me through a center hall toward what proved to be a sunroom. I could hear a slight commotion from below; perhaps the door we'd just passed was a staircase to the kitchens. He gestured awkwardly at a set of chintz-cushioned rattan furniture. "Will you take a seat? There'll be tea."

"Might I wash first?"

"Oh! Bugger, of course."

I nearly laughed again. He couldn't have been more than twenty, and I wouldn't be surprised if he'd found work in Leicester or Birmingham rather than here at ye olde estate. He was surely not a trained footman. "Have you come home to keep your mother safe during this time of uncertainty?" I let the amusement show, but gently.

He must have grasped my intent to reassure. I might, after all, have been anything but a harmless bookworm. He sighed, half-smiled, and gestured again. "There's a proper washroom, sir. Plumbed five years ago, when the old master couldn't manage the stairs anymore. He spent hours a day in here." Another gesture, to the cozy sunroom.

"It's a delightful room. I'll see to myself then, and wait here. Perhaps Mrs. Morris could give me a tour in half an hour?"

"Of course. Thank you sir. I'll just, I'll go." He saw himself out in a fluster.

I bit my lip, collected myself, and went to find the washroom. Good Lord, what unexpected luxury. A basin with hot and cold taps; a separate water closet which included a urinal; and, through a pebbled-glass door, a soaking tub. Elizabeth swore she'd have one in her house as soon as practicable; she would be sick with envy. Up to now, I'd only ever seen one in a house of ill repute in London. Let me add for the record that I was there with a gaggle of damn-fool young men celebrating the imminent marriage of another such, and far too much a coward to avail myself of any services. I had, to be honest, lusted only for the tub.

I lusted for this one. Giving it a look of promise, I employed the urinal, washed my hands and face in blissfully warm water, dried myself with a Turkish towel laid ready, then combed my hair. I'd worn my second-best casual suit, light blue with a gray stripe. Thanks to fine weather, my shoes were free of muck and my collar remained starchily white. Did I look like the owner of a country estate? Well, I *was*.

Thus resolved, I wandered back to the sunroom (tempting though it was to stray) and gazed out the bank of windows over a garden. There were flowers in profusion, some of which I recognized, along with many others I didn't. Trellised roses formed a wall around the garden; beyond those, what might be apple trees. I would have to consult the surveyor's map provided by the executor. This was not a farm per se, but clearly it met at least some of its own needs. And of course Mrs. Morris would be able to answer many questions. If the blasted woman would appear with the promised tea.

Before I had time to convert my parched throat into ill temper, she bustled in, carrying a laden tray. "Mr. Richards, I do apologize for the delay. We knew you were meant to arrive today but not exactly when."

Fair enough. I inclined my head and took a seat. "Much obliged, madam. Perhaps it is not done, but will you sit with me? I've many questions, and I'm a working man myself, so we needn't stand on too much ceremony. You could ring for another cup and plate?" I suggested. She complied, looking somewhat dazed. "I take it the previous owner was more formal."

"More formal," she echoed, taking a seat with an air of deep foreboding. The rattan creaked sympathetically. A few minutes later, a young housemaid appeared bearing a smaller tray, and a few minutes after that the housekeeper relaxed enough to talk. It was an illuminating conversation. She had never worked for anyone other than landed gentry – meaning the only work those people did, unless they served in Parliament, was connected to the estate. This house had been in her charge for twenty years, since shortly after the 'old master' returned, at sixty-five, from a life abroad.

I knew, in a vague way, how much work an estate could be. I did not aspire to become any more of a farmer than my predecessor. "I'll confess," I said, fortified by tea and cakes, "I'd prefer to maintain an office so that I can continue to serve my clients. I'll look into that. But now, might you have time to show me the house?"

"Indeed sir, with pleasure."

She was much more at ease once we were on our feet and moving. The main floor of the house comprised a reception room; a dining room; the sunroom; a study, which contained some mysteries I'd have to return to; the washroom; and what must have served as the old master's chamber once the stairs were beyond him. It was an oddly large room, perhaps originally two, and sparsely furnished. I coveted all that space and had every intention of making it my own master chamber. It was, after all, adjacent to the washroom.

Upstairs, off two separate staircases, were six furnished bedchambers – each with a small dressing room – and a pair of lumber rooms. The attic, I was informed, was occupied only by the two housemaids. The groundsmen bedded down above the stable; the cook and Mrs. Morris had rooms in the basement.

I was slightly appalled. "Was that by choice?"

"Oh yes, sir. Cook's room backs onto the kitchen fire, and mine has its own. We've windows too. You can see if you like."

"No, no. If you're content so am I. Can I say, I am deeply relieved to find so many of the furnishings intact. Faced with entirely empty rooms I might have fled back to Oxford. And it is so nearly ready to entertain."

That won me a smile. "Will you be inviting friends, sir?"

"At the earliest opportunity," I assured her. I could already imagine those upstairs chambers filled with Elizabeth, Sunnam, perhaps even the Duchess. Walpole, of course – mustn't forget him; he'd handed me the place. He and his wife might quite enjoy the occasional week in the country. Their terraced house in Camden used to be the height of my ambition. But this … this was a house I'd be proud to show off to a wife. Perhaps by the time I returned, Sunnam would have news for me.

I spent my first evening in the house – *my* house – writing to my friend.

> My dear Walpole,
>
> There is much to be done at the Leicestershire house, but less than I feared. Tomorrow I'll see the grounds. The staff have made a good first impression; nothing has been neglected since the previous tenant's decease, so far as I can tell.
>
> The very idea of <u>having</u> staff is like a pebble in my shoe; I don't know that I shall ever be entirely comfortable with it.
>
> You can imagine my relief to find the ground floor and basement have gaslight. Each bedchamber has a fireplace, there are

plentiful windows, and it is almost eerily quiet.

Tell Margaret that, now I can house a wife, I am looking about me. My Oxford friends are assisting me with some inquiries, but I should be happy to hear of anyone who may suit me.

One day soon the two of you must visit me here. It is a change of life so complete, and so sudden, that I'll desire frequent reconnection with the familiar.

Wishing you well –

Donald

The following days were full of discoveries. I prowled the house from attics to root cellar, roamed the grounds for hours, sat in the garden with picnic lunches. There was no audible traffic from vehicles; all I could hear were the voices of farm animals, birds, and the household staff. The air bore no pall of coal-smoke; the breeze smelt of fresh bread, mint, and roses.

Had I not, out of habit, brought work with me, I could quite easily have lain completely idle. As it was, I solicited the aid of Henry Morris to shift the big desk in the study closer to a window, which I duly opened. If I then spent five of every ten minutes gazing out at the view instead of working, who could blame me?

Aurelia

The interview with Dr. Gould was, to the extent such a thing can be, delightful. He was a shockingly good-looking man, with lovely manners. The appropriate chaperone was a bright-eyed housemaid with, unless I was sorely mistaken, Ambitions. We met in a library which appeared to be a work in progress; the shelves were a bit more than two-thirds full. I positively itched for a closer look.

Gould first provided a brief biography of his friend, the wife-seeker, without furnishing the man's name. I pretended equanimity at that, telling myself that anyone whose friends had houses like this one was well-advised to limit encroachment. Gould's questions to me had at first mostly to do with my education and intellectual tastes. Then we moved on to my family history and connections; a brief inquiry into travel (brief because the most exotic place I'd ever been was Penzance); and a game of chess. "He was serious, then," I remarked, as my inquisitor set up the pieces.

"Indeed," he murmured, smiling. "My friend has lived all his life in Oxford. He does not wish to flee his home in search of congenial company."

More people should think that way when they consider taking on a spouse. "I was engaged once," I said, when we were each four moves in.

He flicked a glance up at me. "Were you?"

"He was in the Army. Killed in 1899." In one of the first skirmishes of the second Boer war.

"I'm sorry."

"The price of Empire," I said incautiously.

"One of them."

The words were sharp and cold as blades. I glanced up and made eye contact. "Good God, I beg your pardon. I completely forgot –"

He produced some fraction of a smile. "Shall I take that as a compliment?"

"You may if you like, but I hope you'll tell me, should we meet again, how to better conduct myself with citizens of colonial heritage. I've hardly met any, up to now."

"You've not met Mr. LaSalle, then?"

He referred to a gem magnate from Ceylon, cousin to the Marquess of Rowland. "No, but I've heard of him. My last employer's wife wanted to invite him to dinner, by which you may understand she wanted him to meet her daughter. She said, but he's unmarried and owns a sapphire mine, plus he's related to half of Yorkshire. Sir Rupert flatly refused. Does the man not look English?"

"Oh, he does. Not nearly as dark as I. But he takes pride in his background. Says, one day, most of this Empire will revert back to its original owners, and the rest will look like me."

"Ooh, how scandalous." I made another move. "Check."

"Oh, well done." He studied the board, made a move to save his king.

I gloated, the tiniest bit, as I moved my remaining bishop. "Checkmate."

He smacked a hand down on the table, laughing. Toppled his king. Leaned back in his chair. I'd thought all along that I was doing well enough. Now, perhaps, I could actively hope. Before I could say anything, he said, "Sherry? To celebrate your win?"

"Yes, thank you." I watched as he rose, went to the sideboard, unstoppered a decanter, and splashed two fingers of pale golden liquid into each of a pair of cut-crystal glasses. He returned to the table and handed me a glass, then clinked his against it. "Cheers," I said. "Well played."

"Hmph." He sat again, still smiling. "Miss Dashwood, I do believe my friend would like to meet you."

I took a sip – good God, this was the best sherry I'd ever tasted – held it in my mouth for a moment so the aromatics could permeate my brain, then swallowed. "Dr. Gould, I should be genuinely pleased to meet a friend of yours." That was the end of the interview, but not the end of the day. The maid, who'd been visibly bored by the chess game, slipped out of the room; a scant minute later, another person entered. This one went directly to the sideboard and poured herself a glass of the same sherry, then advanced with her right hand extended. I rose, offering mine. "Miss Bonner?"

"The same, Miss Dashwood. I suppose everyone and his dog makes the sense and sensibility joke?"

"Only once each," I said, baring my teeth in a smile. She laughed, raised her glass to me, and took a drink. I returned the salute. "Thank you for hosting this meeting. Have you known Dr. Gould's friend very long?"

"Oh, mercy, I haven't known *anybody* very long; I only moved to England last year. But he was one of the first friends I made in Oxford, so I'm happy to help. Also I'm insatiably curious –"

"Nosy," Gould murmured.

She narrowed her eyes at him. "What I *meant* to say was, the opportunity to meet new people, especially those who might one day become friends, doesn't come my way often enough. So of course I offered my house."

I said, "I'd love to hear more of how you came to England."

"I'd love to tell you! Can you stay for dinner?"

Dinner led to after-dinner tea (a delicious herbal blend with mint), by which time it was so late that Miss

Bonner wouldn't hear of sending me back to London. So I stayed the night.

In the morning, the same housemaid appeared at my door with a tray bearing a pot of chocolate. I sat by the window overlooking Miss Bonner's kitchen garden, with the River Cherwell just visible in the distance, sipping nearly-erotic luxury. The view was a tantalizing reminder of country life. I wondered if the solicitor's house was on the water. Not much later, I was offered my own linens – somehow cleaned and dried overnight while I slept on a featherbed, under a quilt pieced from a dozen exotic velvets, in someone else's calico nightgown – and invited to breakfast downstairs.

Eventually, of course, I made my way to the train station, and thence back to reality. My heart wanted to pour itself out in a letter to my mother; she'd been nearly as grief-stricken as I when Alistair was killed, but much less resigned to what had then seemed likely to be my permanent spinsterhood. If she knew I was negotiating for a husband, she'd be beside herself. But if it didn't come off, she'd be crushed.

I wished I knew what the solicitor looked like. It was highly unlikely that he was anywhere near as handsome as Dr. Gould, but at least there was a good chance he was close to my own age. I was nothing special myself, after all. It was immaterial. At worst I'd had a fine day and night out in Oxford. At best … well, anything was possible.

Donald

Upon my return to Oxford, a message at my rooms informed me that I was to attend Miss Bonner immediately, unless actual business claimed my attention. Which it did, so after a discontented night's sleep (the noise of the city had never seemed so obnoxious) I disposed of the most urgent items before strolling across town.

"I do hope you have nothing else to do for the rest of the day," Elizabeth said as I walked into her library. "Because Sunnam's seen two dozen prospective brides and I've seen half of those, and we have *so very much* to discuss."

I stared at her, nonplussed. "Could we not begin with the house?" No doubt I sounded plaintive. I was big with news and, while earnestly interested in the fact that *so many women* had replied, would confess to something more than nerves concerning my future dwelling.

"Of course we will," Sunnam told me, with an exasperated glance at Elizabeth. "Sherry?"

"Whisky," I suggested hopefully. A few minutes later we were comfortably disposed around the library table. I swallowed some of the fiery liquor, settled my breath, and gave them a summary of my recent observations. "It's more than I ever imagined for myself. A proper house, with a bit of land. Well, you've seen the surveyor's map." They both nodded, with an air of suppressing questions. "There's nothing but good to say about the buildings or the staff. It's the maintenance that frightens me." Now they exchanged a look. "There is no income from the property per se. There are shares, and some other investments, that've produced sufficient income to pay the staff and keep the roof tiles on. But Lizzie, I'll need advice on how to produce *more* income, because there's not been much left over and all I know of money is a few hundred pounds in the Bank of England."

She blinked, nodded, and said, "Would you consult Marius? Because he's the one managing mine. Drafts all the letters to my bankers and brokers, tells me when to sell shares or when to raise rents."

"How's he know all that?"

"Naturally gifted. He was at hand when my inheritance came to me and helped me sort through everything. You should have seen the executor's face." She made big eyes at us. "Took me down to Wall Street to meet with someone he knew. Fascinating to learn, but infinitely tedious to manage. Fortunately when I asked if he'd like to, he said yes."

I had no objections. Lizzie clearly wasn't short of funds, and I wasn't likely to find a better financial advisor nearer to hand, or with a greater incentive to serve me well. So she went out, and a few minutes later returned with Marius. We shook hands and I told him about my concerns. We agreed on a day to meet so he could see all the paperwork I'd accumulated. "Much obliged," I said. "I shouldn't like to propose to anyone until I know we truly will have enough to live on."

"Will you keep up with your practice?" Elizabeth sipped her sherry and eyed me.

"Perhaps? If I learn to ride, I could take an office in Coventry. I honestly don't aspire to bucolic toil, wouldn't know what to do with complete leisure, and, well. The law is all I've ever done."

She patted my knee. "I understand perfectly. Once you've made plans with Marius, perhaps we can bring in the rest of our joint mind and consider the question of income. But now may we please talk about women?"

Sunnam snorted a laugh into his glass. I shot him an amused glance. Marius excused himself, giving

Sunnam a discreet caress on his way to the door. After a moment, I said, "Twenty-four? Really?"

"The advertisement ran for four days. We received over a hundred letters," Sunnam said.

"What?!"

"It made me sad," Elizabeth said, with an air of confession. "To think so many women would throw themselves at a complete stranger. I've always felt lucky, knowing I need never fear for my security, but it's never been brought home to me in quite such a way."

I was still stuck on, "A hundred?"

"Most were obviously unsuitable for you, some unsuitable for any position in a professional household," Sunnam said. "Half a dozen of the others, I directed to posts on the notice board at the Equatorial. A friend of mine hired one, and the Duchess hired another. Then I held two dozen interviews, and of those, as I said, there are twelve we think you could speak to."

"The twelve I met," Elizabeth put in. "All but two currently reside in London."

I said faintly, "And the others?"

"One in Bristol and the other in York."

"Goodness, she came a long way. What was she like?"

"Thirty-four, a widow, currently keeping house for a headmaster whose wife would prefer someone older, or at least less comely."

That cattish comment made me smile. "Is she?"

"Oh yes. Fine light hair, blue eyes, good complexion. Her chess game is reportedly worse than mine and she's never been on a horse, but she's bright enough."

Something about Lizzie's tone made me say, "You didn't quite like her."

"Well," she hedged, "not for *you*. It's only that I know you rather well and, hmm."

From this I understood the woman to be either a prude or a racialist. "I trust your judgement. I'll write to her if you wouldn't mind sending it over your signature, Sunnam?"

"Not at all." He made a note. "While the young lady from Bristol was in some ways promising, I thought her not quite up to your conversational standard. Shipping family; they didn't send her to school. She works in the business and would prefer not to marry a sailor."

"What she needs is some time in a City household, and a proper dowry," Elizabeth said bluntly. "Fairchild said she'd attend to that if you don't care to meet the girl."

"I think not. Thank you." Ten possible meetings was still a lot, but if they were all in London, "Perhaps I should take rooms in a good hotel, and meet all the others over a day or two?"

Elizabeth sputtered with laughter. "Two, for God's sake! You'll be exhausted." Then she returned to an earlier topic. "Why could you not practice from your home?"

Ah, the perfect opening. "Well," I said judiciously, "the house is not quite convenient to the nearest town, though there is an adequate study. Fully furnished, in fact, if a bit distractingly. You see," I paused for dramatic effect, "there are dragons."

Elizabeth squealed at the same moment Sunnam said, "I beg your pardon?" in the way that meant 'I can't have heard you correctly.'

Then Elizabeth said "Dragons?!" as I fell about laughing.

Once I managed to compose myself I knocked back the last mouthful of whisky. "The old master, it seems, spent a little over forty years abroad. He collected certain things. The staff don't know who made the dragons. They're chimerae. Taxidermy, combining parts of different animals," I explained to Elizabeth, who looked equal parts revolted and fascinated. "Three of them, and they're really quite beautiful in their way. Each is in a glass case on a plinth with a drawer below. I've found the keys to two of the drawers, but not the third." Then I paused again. Elizabeth made an impatient querying noise. "Gemstones, my dear. Mostly of types I barely recognize as such. Yes," forestalling her imminent speech. "Mr. LaSalle was the first person I thought of."

"But you can't open one of the drawers?"

"They're faced with lovely burlwood veneer. I didn't want to have at it with a letter knife."

"Fairchild could probably open it," she mused. I nearly started laughing again. She waved a hand at me. "Why don't you have another drink and read those dozen letters? We'll leave you in peace. Then you could ask us any questions you might have, over dinner."

I think I might be forgiven a frisson of hope that dinner would extend to some congenial private activity; I wasn't married yet, after all. But by the time I finished reading the letters, the mood had passed. "You're right," I said, straightening the edges of the shallow stack. "A bit sad."

Lizzie set her book aside. "Were there any that struck you as simply too desperate?"

The truth was, the entire enterprise was desperate; on my side as well as theirs. I shook my head. "I'll meet all the London ladies."

"Then let me order dinner. Sunnam and I can give you our opinions, and tomorrow you'll arrange the rest."

"I'll contact the ladies for you, if you like," Sunnam said. "Once you know where you'll be staying."

"I can't tell you how much I appreciate your help."

"It's been instructive." He smiled a little. "Ashvi and I have talked for hours."

I'd've loved to know what she thought of all this. A few years older than Sunnam but equally attractive, she must have received offers. Obviously none had been the right kind, or the right person. What I said next must have seemed a complete non sequitur. "If I were part of this household, it would take a catapult to get me out."

Lizzie and Sunnam both laughed, and I felt better.

Aurelia

Receiving the telegram with an appointment time was equal parts annoying and exciting. Annoying because of the assumption that my time was at the Oxford Gentleman's disposal. Which it was, of course, because I would hardly accept a position as governess when a position as wife might be available. I'd a job on the line now, at least, so if this meeting ended with a handshake and goodbye I would have little time to regret it.

After wiring my agreement, I went to a hairdresser. I'd been trimming my own for years, saving the indulgence for just such an opportunity. The following day I received a letter.

> Dear Miss Dashwood,
>
> I write to advise that I will be speaking with ten ladies (out of more than a hundred) over two days, which means our time together will be brief. Please feel free to write me care of the hotel with any specific questions or concerns to be addressed during our appointment.
>
> I look forward to meeting you.
>
> Best regards,
>
> Donald Richards

Did I have specific questions or concerns? Indeed I did. The invitation to bring those to his attention was a surprise.

And now I had his name. I dashed off a note to my brother asking if he'd ever heard of this chap, and might I drop in for tea. He responded with adequate promptness, and I made my way to his rooms.

I had been in London for nearly three months now. You may infer, from the fact that my brother did not invite me to share his lodgings during my stay in the city, that we are not the closest of friends. I was nonetheless unprepared for my current enterprise to meet with derision. As I considered his words, I drank the remaining tea in my cup, making a great show of my composure. Then I set the saucer aside and said, "By what standard do you measure dignity, Ernest? Is it truly less dignified to seek some domestic connection than to live alone in a serviced room unto death?"

He blinked at me, blustered for a moment, and started to say something that began with "For heaven's sake, Aurelia," at which point I interrupted him.

"My dear oblivious brother. Has it never occurred to you that if I were a man, *I* might have read law? *I* might have taken rooms in Gray's Inn and been called to the Bar? *I* might now contemplate a profitable union with a respectable young person, leading to a life of domestic comfort? Instead I have spent the past dozen years in four positions of mild but genuine servitude, all of which conduce not to domestic comfort, to say nothing of a secure old age, but to mere repetitions of the same *until I die*."

"But Aurelia –"

"Stow it," I snapped. "Our father once gave a sermon on 1 Corinthians, do you remember? Better to marry than to burn? Well, you don't need to marry, do you? You can take your ease with your fetching landlady, or with that doe-eyed clerk of yours for all I know, but I can have *nothing* without marriage. Nothing but ruin and shame. I am thirty years old. I want a man in my bed. Am I to burn away to a shriveled husk? Am I never to hold my own child? *Dignity*?" I might have been screeching a bit.

"I didn't mean –"

"A rifle ended my first chance at marriage. Now I have a one in ten chance of making a connection with a gentleman of property, an educated man, one who cares enough for his prospective wife to ask her to specify her concerns. How dare you even think, let alone say, that I am *better off* a spinster!"

Apparently done, I sat there, panting and wet-eyed, while he stared at me with his mouth open. After an awfully silent moment, he swallowed, cleared his throat, and said, "I beg your pardon. You're quite right."

"I KNOW." Goodness, that was loud.

He made a helpless sort of uncoordinated gesture. If he was this inarticulate in the courtroom, he'd not much of a career ahead of him. But he pulled himself together. "I should have said, several of my colleagues know of the man and a few know him personally. They say he's pleasant, well-mannered, of a temperate disposition, and an excellent lawyer."

I huffed out a breath. "What does he look like?"

"Mmm, nobody mentioned it."

That likely meant there was nothing memorably grotesque about the man, which was cheering. I saw no profit in continuing the topic since Ernest had never met the Oxford Gentleman. I asked instead if he'd been to the theatre lately, and by the time I left we were, if uneasily, friends again.

When the appointed day arrived, I was determined to leave nothing to chance. I'd sent a letter with a few questions and concerns, as suggested. I'd made lists. I'd written out my thoughts on country life, aware that my current longing for it was at least in part a product of my discontent with the city. I'd also written a brief history of my first engagement, which I proposed to leave with Richards to consider during his deliberations. There were, after all, infinite reasons why a lady might not marry; some of those reasons amounted to 'because she doesn't want to.' I'd wanted to. It was, I thought, something he should know.

The hotel's concierge made me welcome. I was conducted without delay to an upstairs room, in which I found a genteel person emitting an aura of chaperonage. Nervous as I was, I nearly laughed. Then the Oxford Gentleman himself entered from an adjoining chamber. I'll admit this was a hopeful assumption, borne on the wings of startled delight: he was *not at all* grotesque.

He advanced, one hand extended, wearing a pleasant smile with his well-made suit. "Miss Dashwood?"

"Mr. Richards?" We shook hands. "Has this experience been too terribly exhausting?"

He huffed out a laugh, indicating a pair of wingback chairs set either side of a low table. "My best friend in Oxford is a woman, and she told me it would be. Miss Elizabeth Bonner, late of America, who met with you."

I took my seat, affecting nonchalance. "She was very kind to me."

"She liked you," he said, which surprised me. "As did Dr. Gould."

"He was lovely. Were you at university together?"

"Indeed we were."

We talked very briefly of Oxford; I mentioned my brother's time at Cambridge; my host offered tea, which I declined. "This late in the day, sir, I venture to guess I may be your last appointment?" He made a sound of assent. "In which case you're likely awash with tea. I do hope you've nothing you must do this evening but sit and be quiet."

He was openly smiling; it suited him. "You've hit upon my exact plan. You are, in fact, the last of all my appointments. There was a reason." He stopped there, which didn't suit me at all. I made an inquiring noise and a get-on-with-it gesture. He bit his lip – did he mean for me to look at his mouth? – and said, "I wanted to see all the others before you, because I thought I would like you best, but if I saw you first I might not be fair to them."

Good God. I performed a lightning-fast survey of face, breath, hands: was I composed? At least externally. "May I ask why you thought you'd prefer me?"

"Because of my friends' observations. And your letters."

"I wrote another one," I confessed. "I meant to leave it with you this evening, if we got on. But perhaps I could tell you a story or two instead?" He looked so relieved that I finally relaxed. Without further ado, I told a story about leaving school and going back home to my parents. Having The Talk about my options. What they could give me, and what they couldn't, and the subsequent decision to seek employment. Then I told a story about meeting Alistair, while supervising the offspring of a young mother during the Season. That ended, of course, with Alistair's mother's letter to me, telling me he'd been killed.

Donald's eyes were soft with sympathy. "I'm so sorry."

"It was a difficult time," I admitted. "The life I'd begun to plan for was suddenly out of my reach. Were you ever engaged?"

He shook his head. "My family is much like yours, genteel but not wealthy. My father was a merchant; he died while I was at university, and my mother now lives with her brother. There was not much of a legacy, only enough to establish myself and to provide my sister a small jointure. I thought there was a chance I might seek a wife by forty." He smiled faintly at my inadvertent exclamation. "Instead here I am, at thirty-two, attempting to grasp a future for which I am wholly unprepared."

We gazed at each other for a moment. I knew what he was seeing: an averagely-pretty woman, not old but no longer in the bloom of youth, with straight brown hair and blue eyes. The new dress flattered me; it was a deep russet color with a thread of duck-egg blue, and the seamstress had made a good job of fitting it. I thought I might be forgiven for thinking we were well-matched. He was averagely-handsome, not very tall, and his light-brown hair was unlikely to see him to fifty. But his complexion was pale and clear, the bones of his face promised a distinguished old age, and his eyes were beautiful. I meant to say something complimentary about his friends. How fortunate he was to have people willing to help him grasp that future. Instead I said, "We could make a success of it." And he smiled again.

Donald

Had I not been truly fatigued, well aware that I needed to let my thoughts settle, I might have invited Miss Dashwood to dine with me that evening. Instead I inquired as to her plans to following night. She said she had none. I proposed dinner and the theatre. She accepted with evident pleasure and gave me her direction. I promised to arrive in a suitable conveyance at a certain time, and went to bed feeling, it must be said, hopeful. Also discontented with my virtuously solitary bed. It was, at least, a much finer bed than my own.

In the morning, I sat down with all the letters and all my notes, giving nine of the women a chance to alter my conviction. None managed it. As directed by the Duchess, I wrote up a summary of my impressions. She'd promised to tug upon her web to find better situations for the candidates I must dismiss. Then I dashed off notes to Sunnam and Elizabeth, shaved and dressed, and went to consult my banker.

That gentleman treated me differently these days, which might've annoyed me had I not thoroughly understood him. We all had only so much time and attention to give; I was worth more of his now. C'est la vie. After our consultation, I went to a jeweler.

Thanks (again) to Lizzie and her social connections, 'jeweler' did not mean 'pawnshop.' It also did not mean Bond Street or other Society environs. The shop was in a pleasant enclave, a village within the city, bounded by terraced houses. I presumed most of them were occupied by the families of professionals and merchants. In any case, the jeweler showed me a number of items appropriate to my new station, did not attempt to sell me any gaudy trifles, and congratulated me on my intent.

I had then some time remaining, and chose to spend it (along with a few more pounds) in a bookshop. Errands done, I returned to the hotel; washed and dressed for the evening; and, impatiently, waited.

When I arrived at her lodgings, Miss Dashwood came promptly to the door, wearing an evening dress – pale pink with russet embroidery, an India paisley shawl draped over her shoulders. Her hair was up, with a pink diamanté flower pinned above one ear. She did not look as though she'd spent the day weighing second thoughts. Set her hand in mine, stepped up into the carriage, arranged her skirts, and smiled. "I've been so excited all day."

I smiled back. "As have I. Not in the mood for tragedy, I hope?"

"Good heavens, no. What will we see tonight?"

"The Pirates of Penzance."

"Ooh!" She actually clapped her hands. "I saw it years ago, in Brighton. Drove my entire school mad humming the songs for a week."

"There was a time my friends and I plagued the taproom of our favorite pub with unsolicited performances of With Catlike Tread," I told her as the carriage lurched into motion. She laughed. I reached for her hand. She let me hold it all the way to the restaurant.

Having personal experience mostly of pub dining, I'd leant on Lizzie and the Duchess again for advice. Since our theatre for the night was in the West End, I'd arranged to dine at J Sheekey. Miss Dashwood seemed to enjoy the buttery fish pie, and I enjoyed simply everything. She was such good company, and it seemed so unforced. At ease and quick-witted; friendly, but willing to argue a point; lovely to look at.

I was not, you understand, inexperienced with women. Aside from my recent liaison with Elizabeth I had, over the years, dined with, walked out with, and gone to the theatre with a fair few others. Thus my basis for comparison. My intent was always to go into this endeavor with an open mind, to be objective, and to have the future always in my sights. It was ever so slightly lowering to realize that I might've been inclined to make excuses for Miss Dashwood. To think, we can work around this, or we can compromise on that. But in truth? No excuses were required. I thought we could make a success of it.

Because my friends were determined that I should be seen in the best possible light, the Duchess made her box at the theatre available to me. Miss Dashwood entered with what I began to recognize as her characteristic composure. No doubt she'd been in boxes before, as the person in charge of a wealthy family's adolescent representatives. The attendant in the box circle closed the door behind us. I removed my hat and laid it on the small table by the door; we took our seats; we divested ourselves of gloves. I smoothed mine before laying them on my lap, glancing up to see her watching. "I rarely wear them."

"Tell me about a day in the life of a solicitor."

I blinked, surprised; but then I understood. I rarely wore gloves because I spent my days meeting people indoors, shaking hands, leafing through documents, and writing. While the theatre filled up and the noise level rose, I told her of my routine, with a few illustrative anecdotes. Then the great gasoliers over the house dimmed, and the orchestra began to play. We both turned to face the stage for the national anthem.

The difference between sitting in the stalls with a mere friend and sitting in a box with one's intended bride is, simply, enormous. The small, enclosed space gave us a modicum of privacy. No one shuffled past or behind us; if our nearest neighbors talked through the performance, I could not hear them. I was acutely aware of Miss Dashwood's presence. She wore a delicate scent, unfamiliar to me. Every laugh made me smile; every sound of appreciation went directly to my prick.

Had we met in the usual sort of way, I'm sure I would have liked her just as well. Having met with the express intention of marriage (that is, leaving aside all the prevarication and coyness attending a social acquaintance) seemed to have muted my chronic self-deprecation. I did not have to ask myself if she was interested: I knew she was. Moreover, I knew her better than I'd known any woman but Lizzie. By issuing this invitation, I'd as good as offered marriage. By accepting, she'd as good as said yes. When I was not actively watching and listening to the performance, I was rehearsing my speech for later. Wondering when to make it. There was no point carrying on as if we were undecided. And there was really no point waiting until I took her home. Or perhaps I simply didn't wish to.

During the interval, after each of us returned from our respective retiring rooms, I told her about the letters I'd sent. Then the attendant brought in a bottle of champagne, with a pair of crystal glasses, and Miss Dashwood's eyes went wide. We said nothing while the bottle was opened and the wine poured. When the attendant had gone I offered a glass; she accepted; I lifted mine. "Miss Dashwood, I would be less precipitate had we met in the usual way. However, we did not, and I believe we both have reason to move forward as quickly as possible. You are everything I could wish for in a wife. Shall we yoke ourselves together, and make a success of it?"

I could see the wish to tease me in her eyes, but she bit her lip. Did she know how that drew my attention to her mouth? She lifted her glass to tap it against mine. "Mr. Richards, I think we shall." We each drank, betraying our mutual nerves by draining the glasses. I set them aside and took her hand. Kissed the back of it, then turned it over to kiss the delicate skin of her wrist. Heard the sudden intake of breath that told me she was moved. Folded her hand between mine and held it to my lips, gazing into her eyes. The second act was beginning, but I heard nothing. When I dropped my hands (still holding hers) to my lap I lowered my gaze, but my attention was all on the feel of her skin against mine.

It was not until With Catlike Tread that I let go of her and dug in my coat pocket for the ring. It took both hands to open the blasted box. "I know this is not the time," I murmured, "but on the day."

She stared at the modest ring – a white gold band with a filigree cartouche set with a small, brilliant diamond – and said, "Oh, Donald."

I liked my name on her tongue; she said it the way I preferred, with a longish O and a muted terminal D. "May I call you Aurelia?"

"Of course."

We did not kiss then, but only because hundreds of people could see us. We waited until we were in the carriage. In between kisses, I suggested that we could go to Somerset House to register the next day. From there, we would remove to Oxford: I to my lodgings, and Aurelia to Elizabeth's house. "We can have the ceremony in a local church, or at home, whichever you prefer."

"You're certain Miss Bonner won't mind?"

I kissed the worry from her face. "My dear, I would never hear the end of it if you were to stay anywhere else till we can finalize our union."

"I'm glad enough to leave London," she said. "I must write to my parents. They may wish to come."

"Of course. My mother too. We can talk about all that on the train."

"Yes. My goodness, Donald. We really mean to marry." It was almost a question.

"I am determined," I told her. "I could be satisfied with no other." She took my meaning: because we met, none of the others would do. She pressed close and kissed me again.

I have said that I was not inexperienced with women. Thus I could say, with some confidence, that my attraction to Aurelia was honestly reciprocated. And – much to my delight – openly expressed. She did not merely sit and receive my kisses. It was her hand, not mine, that strayed to undo my waistcoat buttons, sliding beneath to press against my chest. The one remaining layer of clothing felt a damn sight too many. Especially with her mouth hot on the bare skin below my ear.

I was truly, madly, *deeply* discontented with my solitary bed that night.

As it happened, all of our parents suggested that the newlyweds might visit them instead, which suited me and Aurelia. "This way you'll get to see my parents' home, and I'll get to see Shrewsbury," she said. "And meet your sister's family."

"I've not been to Brighton for years." Even those prosaic excursions sounded like great adventures to me; perhaps she felt the same. *Everything* was exciting. We kept reaching for each other. Holding hands, sitting shoulder-to-shoulder and thigh-to-thigh. Kissing, whenever we were alone. Elizabeth, unsurprisingly, provided us many opportunities to be alone. No doubt I could have given up all claim to propriety and spent the nights with Aurelia, had we not firmly and repeatedly stated our intention of doing otherwise. It was necessary to so state, you understand, because otherwise we would have fallen on each other like starving dogs on a saddle of mutton.

I dined at Chez Bonheur every night, except the night I hosted a gathering at my favorite pub. When my day was not entirely spoken for, I went to Lizzie's early. Sometimes I spoke with Marius about my financials; sometimes everyone in the house convened in the library to discuss what one did with a country house.

"I've had a thought on that subject," Elizabeth said, "but I really need to see the place before I say anything."

"That must be killing you," Marius said, to a stifled snort from Sunnam.

She glared at them both. Aurelia was giggling with Ashvi, with whom she'd been spending a great deal of time. She told me it was to resurrect her culinary skills, it having been years since she had access to a proper kitchen. My reminder that there was no need – my house came with a cook, after all – was airily dismissed. "I *like* knowing my way around a kitchen, darling." She'd learned very quickly that calling me 'darling' melted me completely.

Four weeks from the day we registered, our union was solemnized. We would not stay with Elizabeth that night; the Duchess had offered a suite of rooms, quite private, in a little-used corner of her house. Elizabeth had taken Aurelia along several times when she called on Fairchild, so she was accustomed to the fact of knowing a Duchess. She was accustomed to being served, rather than a servant, though there was little enough distinction at Lizzie's. Most importantly, neither of us had, over the past twenty-eight days, discovered any reasons to regret our decision. Only the fact that we must exit Elizabeth's carriage in daylight kept us from committing various improprieties en route.

Aurelia

We saw no one but Fairchild's imposing butler Amon. He conducted us gravely through the entry hall, up the stairs, down a corridor to what would be our rooms for the next two nights. Advised us that we had only to ring and the household would supply any comfort we found lacking. The study on the far side of the dressing room was set for our dinner, which would be served at seven o'clock. He saw himself out with a bow. Seconds later, a footman tapped and requested permission, which we duly granted, to deliver our bags.

Left alone, we drifted into the suite. Through to inspect the study (which was indeed set for dinner), returning to the dressing room to inspect its private washroom, then to the bedroom again. A fire was burning, though little needed; I felt ready to combust. "It is only five o'clock," I said after a moment. "There are doubtless a hundred things we should speak of."

"Or only one," Donald said, approaching. He set his hands on my shoulders and drew me close. "Aurelia, my wife. Would you wait till after dinner, or may I take you to bed now?"

"Now," I said softly. "Now is good." We laughed into the kiss.

I had not asked Donald if he expected me to seek counsel about the marriage bed. My mother, of course, provided some. Past conversations with married friends provided more. And then there was Elizabeth. She was unmarried, and younger than I. But the members of her household were not, shall we say, reserved when in private. A few days of mounting confusion, followed by a few days of growing comprehension, had led me to several conclusions. Firstly: Marius and Sunnam were lovers. Secondly: Marius and Elizabeth were lovers. Finally: Elizabeth and Donald were, or had been, lovers. That 'finally' refers, you understand, to those within the home. For aught I knew, all of them had additional lovers elsewhere. I would have laid odds that if any did, it was Elizabeth; her conduct with the Duchess (as manly a woman as I had ever seen, and I mean that as a compliment) supported that conclusion.

At first I was shocked. I was brought up in a vicar's household: taught that certain things were right and others wrong, and never the twain shall mix. I thought I should be appalled. But I questioned my preconceptions, as I lay on my comfortable bed in that quiet house. Did I find any of these people ill-suited to the others? No. Did I, in point of fact, care if a man loved another man, or a woman another woman? No. Did I truly give a toss if unmarried people engaged in sexual congress? No. I'd've done it myself if I could have borne the risk.

Elizabeth could bear the risk. She was independent, rich, and surrounded by people who not only loved her, but formed a protective phalanx about her. People who were, plainly, not jealous or possessive. Instead of wondering why she might indulge with more than one person, I held my peace and observed, gradually coming to see that each person was so distinct from the others as to provide some unique ingredient essential to the feast of love that was this household. I had no doubt that if Elizabeth were to conceive, all of them together would bring up the child. It would want for nothing except, perhaps, complete respectability. But that was none of my concern. There was only one thing that concerned me.

I waited until we lay gasping side by side, my body hot, slick, and aching; Donald's a delicious symphony of hair, sinew, sweat, and musk. Was it perfect bliss? Not quite; there was some discomfort. I had every confidence that our next attempt would be even better. I turned my head, clawed my disorderly hair off my face, and pressed a kiss to his shoulder. "May I ask you something?"

"Of course, darling."

"Do you intend to continue bedding Elizabeth?" He made a stifled sort of gasping noise, as if he'd been hit. I patted him randomly, then let my fingertips trail through the hair beneath them. "I ask only so that I can govern myself accordingly. I don't desire any of my new friends except you. But I understand why you might –"

"Aurelia, I beg of you." He lurched up, propping himself on one elbow, gazing down at me with alarm that was clear even in the dim light of a single lamp. "Believe that I have not, ahem, with Elizabeth since we decided I should marry."

I almost laughed. "Since *we* decided?"

"Well, she told me I should." Still staring at me, eyebrows drawn together in puzzlement. "Did she tell you about …?"

"Oh no. None of them breathed a word. But only a fool could live a month in that house and fail to see." He sank back down on the bed, though with one arm across my body and one leg between mine. Claiming me? I quite liked it. Liked everything about it, from the hairy shin to the thumb caressing my ribs, and the soft insistence of his parts pressed to my hip. “I would prefer to cleave only unto you,” I said. “And vice versa.”

“I have sworn to forsake all others,” he said, holding me tight. “And I shall.”

“Excellent.” I patted him again, less randomly. “We can speak of other things while we dine. It must be nearly six.”

So it proved, which left time for a good wash, after which I donned my new nightgown (a gift from Ashvi) and dressing gown (a gift from Elizabeth). Then I sat before the mirror and watched as Donald combed out my hair. I offered to braid it; he said he preferred it down. He bent to kiss me, then walked – splendidly nude; the man stripped to advantage – across the room to find his pyjamas. “I have never before dined with a lady while wearing pyjamas,” he informed me as he pulled open the study door. “If I find it as comfortable as I expect, we may have set a dangerous precedent.”

“Imagine how comfortable I am, without a corset. Or drawers.” He twitched at the reminder. I gave him a wicked smile and reclined on the chaise, watching a parade of servants bringing covered dishes, opening a bottle of wine, lighting candles, then quietly departing.

A leisurely two hours later we left the detritus of a brilliant meal behind us, closed the door between study and washroom, and made ourselves ready for bed. “This will be the first time I’ve shared a bed since school,” I said, wriggling between the sheets. Wincing slightly.

He must have been watching; he gathered me close and kissed me. “I trust you’ll push me out of bed if I snore.”

I thought about it for a few seconds, then shook my head. “Mmm, no, but I reserve the right to give you a hearty thump."

"Fair enough. Ignore that," he added.

I pressed my hip against his parts, acknowledging their interest in another bout. "That?"

"Wicked! You must be sore. I can wait."

"Mmm, no," I said again. "I might wait, with thanks, for an exact repetition. But tell me what else we can do."

"Oh! Really? Well, there's this." He moved my hand. What followed was sufficiently inspiring that, after, he held me against him, mouth on the back of my neck, and used his hand as productively as ever I'd used mine.

I gave him his wedding gift, a fine new fountain pen, in the morning. Then he suggested another way of loving, which began with his mouth on me and, once I'd thoroughly recovered from the shock, progressed to mine on him; it was glorious. I might have sung Poor Wand'ring One in the bath. Donald might have hummed Oh Is There Not One Maiden Breast while he combed my hair again. We strolled in Fairchild's garden, then fled blustery rain and retreated to her conservatory. We had coffee with her, talking lazily about her intention to travel to India. Mr. Salazar, Fairchild's secretary, indicated that he might accompany her; then she mentioned that Elizabeth also meant to go. "Which means Marius and likely Sunnam, so we might as well charter our own bloody boat," she said, with a notable lack of irritation. "Mr. LaSalle may come along."

"That's quite a party," I said. "Purely for pleasure?"

"Severin, Mr. LaSalle that is, has business," Fairchild said. "He's been absent from Ceylon for over a year."

"He'll be back from France soon," Salazar murmured.

I must have displayed interest. Fairchild said, "Has Lizzie told you about the case of the bloody thief?"

"She did. Oh! Agatha Fletcher went to France. Is that?" I let the question trail off.

Fairchild nodded. "Agatha's friend Catriona is a gifted illustrator. She's preparing the artwork for a book Severin means to publish. The memoir of his ancestor who lived in Ceylon a hundred years ago. He mentioned wanting to get the paintings to his engraver before we left England."

That led to a brief discussion of an illustrated book Donald acquired in London, and then to an invitation to make free of Fairchild's library before retiring to our rooms. We dined there privately again, this time discussing the new clothes that I must have, and how best to budget for them. Then we went to bed, where no clothes at all were needed. Or wanted.

We each wrote to our mothers in the morning, telling of the wedding and our modest honeymoon, then adding postscripts to each other's letters so that our families should hear from both of us. I could not, of course, write 'thank you for producing such a completely satisfactory man' to the elder Mrs. Richards; nor could I hint to my mother of the things I meant to say the next time we were private together.

You may infer that 'how did I live without this for so long' would be among those things.

There followed a period of weeks during which many letters were sent and received. Donald proposed to keep his office in Oxford only until new digs in Coventry could be secured and his clients duly notified.

His rooms – a fine example of 'bookish single gentleman's flat' – required no improvement since we were so shortly to move on.

I was left with swaths of unoccupied time, a luxury of the purest sort. I spent hours roaming Oxford, hewing to a strict budget in the bookshops. More hours were spent at Chez Bonheur, at Elizabeth's invitation. Her study hours were inviolate, but Ashvi welcomed me to kitchen and garden. She and Daisy, and sometimes Mary, would sit with me and talk about housekeeping. It might have bored other women, but consider: for years I'd expected never to have my own home. Never to have the right to make even the trivial decision of what should be brought to my table at dinner.

"You are not in the least bored," Elizabeth said one afternoon, when she'd left the library and joined me in the garden for tea.

"Not in the least," I agreed. "I must thank you again for making me free of your home."

"You're most welcome. What shall you have in yours, that I have not?"

"A piano," I said instantly. "My parents have one; I've played since I could toddle."

"Ooh, I never learned." She leaned forward, face bright with interest. "My feminine accomplishments begin and end with how to dress."

I smiled. "You dress beautifully. How did you manage not to be indoctrinated in all the other decorative arts?"

"My mother died when I was young, my father was occupied in business, and my aunts were just distant enough that they didn't realize they should interfere until it was too late." She produced half a shrug, along with a mischievous expression. "By the time they decreed I should put up my hair and join company, no one expected me to have needlework in my hands, or to perform. If I did not hold a book, I expected to converse. My grandfather encouraged me."

"Did he enjoy you, then?"

She took my meaning. "He did. His daughters – my aunts – are good women, but they are the product of their time. I aspired to college; I was interested in his business; nobody else in the family was. I think I was thirteen when he told me how much he valued a willing ear."

"And naturally that made you all the more willing to listen."

"Naturally." She smiled. "That was the age when I realized I wouldn't need womanly accomplishments. We had money. Even if I married, my grandfather would see to it I always had my own funds. I would never need to cook my own meals or launder my own clothes, and if I preferred to spend my evenings with books rather than embroidery, he was the last to object. But you know all those things, don't you? As well as literature, and three languages, and bloody *chess*?"

Her clear admiration made me blush. "My mother is accomplished, my father is educated, and for a time I expected to have the running of my own home. We are the sort of people who mend our own clothes. Bake our own bread. All the rest came with my schooling, discovering I had brains, and then considering how to use them."

"You've said it was after you left school that you really determined on employment."

"Yes. It was," I paused, "not something I feared. It was rather a way for me to see something of the world.

So I wanted to be fit for it." Elizabeth nodded eagerly. How I appreciated her comprehension. After a sip of tea, I said, "My employment added to my store of knowledge. I might, in a decade or so, have found a less itinerant way to make use of it."

"But along came Donald, and now that decade is before you. I really cannot wait to see the new house."

"Oh, Lizzie, you'll love it." We smiled at each other.

Donald

I routinely kept good records, but paid particular attention to the matter during this time. Copies of my personal letters, notes in my private diary, annotated ticket stubs and bills. One day, I told my wife, we would want to reconstruct our first months of marriage; at the present time, the pace of change was wont to obscure the course of events.

My *wife*. I had not understood how completely my life would change once it was not mine alone.

Aurelia told me that she would make no resistance to staying as Elizabeth's (or Fairchild's) guest when we visited Oxford in the future. However, until we fully removed to the country house, we shared my lodgings. Two rooms would suffice for two people who were not overburdened with possessions; and after all, we shared the bed. It was glorious.

In the weeks following our wedding, we paid several short visits to the country house, ordering furnishings where needed (each visit produced some new revelation about how the place might best serve us). We spent a few days with my family in Shrewsbury; they were pleased if unexcited about my new situation, being city folk who thought of country living as akin to prison. Aurelia's parents were another case. I was made very welcome; presented with pride to all of their particular friends; offered the best of everything; and advised that their son had written with congratulations.

Aurelia read the letter, snorted a quiet laugh, and shook her head when I asked why. Later, when we were alone, she told me about their conversation in London. "I don't know that Ernest ever gave a moment's thought to my situation," she said. "But then, I don't suppose most men would."

"I never did," I confessed. "Not until we placed that advertisement, and I saw those letters. Elizabeth had things to say."

"Yes, she did." Aurelia smiled at me. "She said, until women have the same rights as men, we will always be at their mercy. The only power I have, in truth, resides in my freedom to say no. To remain unmarried."

"She told me the same." I was slightly distracted by the soft skin below my wife's ear. She squirmed away with an unconvincing protest about being tickled. I pursued her, offering a firmer kiss. Then I lay there, propped on my elbow, caressing her sweet body. "I think she never actually wanted to marry. But you did."

She laid her hand on mine. "Yes, I did, and not only for security. I wanted this. A companion. A lover. I'm so lucky it was you who placed that advertisement."

"*You're* lucky! Shall I enumerate the uxorious pleasures in which I wallow?" She was laughing, yielding, sighing. I had no other object than to make her sigh.

Eventually, of course, the move was made. Elizabeth et al. promised to come for a week in

September, when the weather should still beckon us outdoors. I had raided my savings to ensure the guest rooms were properly equipped; Aurelia used part of her small jointure (happily delivered by her father upon our visit) to arrange shipment of an upright piano. The instrument itself was ours for the asking, having been recently retired from service at the school of her youth. Once it was delivered and tuned, nearly every evening found us in the reception room. I'd always enjoyed a song, but never learned to play; to have a gifted and willing accompanist in my own home was yet another new luxury. Aurelia wrote to various friends who showered her with sheet music, including nearly the complete works of Gilbert and Sullivan.

The days were spent half in correspondence and reading for my practice, and half exploring (and talking about) the house and its environs. Aurelia attempted the locked drawer in the study, gave it up on the same grounds as I, and began organizing the bookshelves. Integrating our own small collections of books resulted in some stimulating disagreements. "Of course we must arrange things by author," she said patiently, the third time the question arose. "*Not* by title, or, God forbid, by subject."

"But I'm more apt to recall a title," I said peevishly.

"Then I'll make an index," she suggested. "With space for new additions. Acceptable?"

I thought about it; tried to find a flaw; eventually conceded. Of course, by the end of a week, I knew where everything was and claimed we never needed the index at all. She permitted me to see her roll her eyes, but spared me any comment.

Though the one drawer remained inviolate, the others produced some surprises. I had seen only the drawers in situ; Aurelia discovered that removing them revealed an internal latch, pressing which released a door in the front of the plinth. Behind these doors she found disorganized stacks of papers, ranging from bills of lading to letters and drawings. “These must have belonged to the old master,” she said one afternoon as she sat on the study floor, surrounded. “Records of his travels. Why on earth would he have hidden them in such a way?”

“I can’t imagine.” That wasn’t quite true. Obviously each plinth had been custom made to support a given dragon in its glass case. The burl veneer on each drawer front was continued in fine marquetry on the faces of the plinth. The whole of it could not have said more clearly ‘my treasures herein.’ And we discovered, as she sorted and organized the papers, that the old master had not traveled alone. He had, for decades, traveled with another man. Knowing Marius and Sunnam as we did, we could not help but draw certain conclusions. “I positively itch to get at that third drawer,” I admitted one night as we lay in bed speculating.

She laughed. “Where do you itch, darling?” Trailing her fingernails along my skin, applying just the right amount of pressure: enough to tease but not tickle. “Here?”

“Ooh! Yes, there.” Needless to say, we did not pursue our speculations any further that night. We did our best to leave the entire subject alone in the days leading up to our first experience as Host and Hostess. We were, to be frank, nervous.

As Aurelia might say, if you have never faced the head-high hurdle that is ‘housing, feeding, and entertaining your best friends,' you may count your blessings.

Selected Letters

Dear Sunnam,

I direct this to you in the full expectation that everyone else at Chez Bonheur will read it.

Every day is a discovery. Morris (the younger, that is Henry) and his colleagues are teaching me to ride. Since my choice of steed must at present be either the cart horse or the plow horse, there is very little danger and also little comfort. The two choices are, you understand, the same animal, one of substantial height and girth. In due course we will acquire a pair of riding horses. My wife has amply demonstrated her competence. She claims that having established a vocabulary of horse management with the current mount, I will have no difficulty in future. I must admit that there is something quite stirring about ambling the property on horseback; perhaps it is the elevated vantage point.

Does Ashvi keep a root cellar? Aurelia says that ours here is an excellent example. My chief impression at first glance, or rather sniff, was the overwhelming aroma of apples. One supposes that potatoes, beetroot, turnips etc have their own scent, but none to match our primary crop. Only the onions can compete.

Our piano has arrived. All visitors will be invited, if not precisely required, to sing.

Yrs -

D. Richards

Dear Ashvi,

Donald has written to your brother; like his, my letter is to be shared.

Have you ever lived in the country? I had, during my weeks in London, developed considerable nostalgia for it, which is now rewarded. We spend hours outdoors every day. Sometimes riding, more often rambling. Our staff spared us time from their various employments to acquaint us with the Estate. (Modest though it is, it deserves capitalization.)

D tells me he did not understand why a house of this size should require so many people until he grasped the daily demands of kitchen garden, creamery, cider house, poultry, etc on top of marketing, cooking, laundry, and cleaning. There are markets within an easy drive (or ride), but one may not simply walk across the street to the pub.

One of the groundsmen intimated that, were an appropriate hutch to be constructed, he could in short order regularly supply us with fresh rabbit. This project advances. Meanwhile we breakfast very well on the remains of last winter's pig, and dine luxuriously on duck, squab, or pullet.

I was astonished and delighted to find that Cook has an adventurous hand with spices. She was used to turn out curries etc for the old master who learnt to love such things while abroad.

You must know that when Elizabeth et al come to visit, I hope you will come too. If you choose to claim a solitary holiday then instead, I will not take offense – but I will miss you.

Yrs - Aurelia

Dear Marius,

Thank you for yours of the –, concerning your analysis of my shares. I will undertake to regularly read the business and political news, instead of confining myself to the society pages. I wish I could disagree that there will be another war before long; it is too much to expect that the next conflict will be confined to some distant colony. My inherent caution (now amplified by a wish to preserve my inheritance) urges me to divest Cunard and White Star no later than 1910, even if we still enjoy relative peace. I'm sure you're correct that we will see submarines deployed in the next major conflict.

Regarding those three books: I'd seen the Satyricon at university, as no doubt had Sunnam. The Memoirs of Fanny Hill came to my attention when some halfwitted friends were planning a bachelor night. The Dialogues of Luisa Sigea, however, was new to me. All three provide endless entertainment. I will spare my wife's blushes and say only that I thank you.

We are still too new to this life to find it tedious. We do, however, very much look forward to seeing you and the others before long.

Your friend,

D. Richards

Dear Elizabeth,

Your steward and his cher ami sent us three naughty books. Did they tell you? Have you read them? D and I both veer from screaming with laughter to squealing with embarrassment to – well, you can imagine, I'm sure. Not the typical wedding gift but may I say we have had an interesting span of evenings. We are Experimenting.

Aside from that, we have fallen into a comfortable routine. I spend the mornings with members of the staff, learning exactly what they do and how; I am writing everything up as a sort of training manual for the eventual day when Mrs. Morris retires and we must hire someone new. D uses that time for business correspondence. In the afternoons, we go outdoors. Later on we have tea in the music room; then I play, or sometimes we sing together, with whichever of the staff care to join us. One of the maids has a lovely voice; I am teaching her to read music and to play. After dinner we retire to the master bedchamber, there to read. (*Not* a euphemism. Not wholly, at least.)

We do not want a fire of an evening. The headboard has a niche on each side for a lamp; we pull the bedcurtains closed and are very cozy. I knew I would like having a man in my bed. Thank you for steering D to me; he is excellent in ways I did not even know to wish for.

I am very happy.

Your friend,

Aurelia

Dear Aurelia,

It is an enormous pleasure to think of you and Donald so happy. No doubt you would both have made the best of your lives in any case, but how much better it is to have a special person! Isn't it? I remember the early days with Daisy. I'd had a wretched evening at a dinner, having an Absolute Pig flung at my head as a potential husband, bearing up under my aunts' vicious whispers about how I must stop giving myself airs and pretending I could be independent, etc. I arrived home in such a state that Daisy's simple kindness – can you remember a time when you desperately needed a consoling touch? – led to me crying on her shoulder. Well, then I practically begged her to stay with me, and bless the girl, she did. Even if our friendship had never taken a turn, I would have wanted her company. I am not made for solitude.

As usual I have made this all about myself. I'm so pleased for you, truly, the pair of you. One day I will be Aunt Elizabeth and then, oh, there will be Such Frolics!

Ever yours,

E.B.

Dear Elizabeth,

I told Aurelia, in London, that I could not imagine a woman better-suited than she to be my wife. She pleases me in ways I did not even know to wish for. And, having known you, my wishes were extensive.

My life now is an order of magnitude superior to my life of four months ago, never mind a year ago. I wish there were some way for me to repay you for the infinite gift that is your friendship.

Sincerely,

D.R.

Dear Donald,

Let us not make a balance sheet of our connection! You know I hate keeping accounts! Suffice to say that at least fifty percent of the excellencies of my Oxford life were facilitated by knowing you, and that I fully expect at least fifty percent of the pleasures of my future life to be likewise enhanced by your acquaintance. (And Aurelia's – she truly is the ideal woman for you, isn't she?)

I am Simply Wild to see your new Manor.

And your DRAGONS.

Ever yours,

E.B.

p.s. Get out of Bed, you shocking Sybarite, and prepare for Imminent Invasion!!

Aurelia

I was not at all surprised that the entire company, upon arrival, demanded dragons. Elizabeth and Sunnam had used the term liberally ever since Donald dropped it in their ears. Thus Marius, Daisy, Fairchild, and Polly were also fervently interested in seeing what the devil he'd meant. The only things that took higher priority were locating their assigned rooms and then trooping in and out of our very modern, very much beloved washroom. As we assembled in the study, I asked after Fairchild's secretary. "I trust Señor Salazar is well?"

"Very well," the Duchess said. "He sends his thanks for the invitation but cannot tear himself from Severin's clutches." Marius snorted with laughter; Sunnam probably blushed; all of the other women joined me in a bland pretense of no-need-for-details. Then I asked Elizabeth about Ashvi.

"Also sends thanks, but she's not had a full week free of me for quite some time and she means to enjoy it." She shrugged, then sent an amused glance at Ashvi's brother. "Free of *us*, I should say."

Sunnam nodded meekly. We all affected not to notice the way he leaned on Marius. Then Mrs. Morris led a parade of servants bringing refreshments into the study; her son Henry brought chairs from the reception room so that everyone could be seated; and the dragons were introduced.

"We still don't know what that one's made of," Donald said, pointing to the blue dragon. "That's the drawer we can't open. But we found the details for the others. This one," he indicated the black dragon, "is a cormorant, with a fox's teeth, extra feet, and feathers from what must've been a dozen cockerels. This," he indicated the green dragon, "is a young crocodile. Its wings are from a green macaw and the color here is butterfly wings. The crest is a dorsal fin."

"This work is stunning," Fairchild said, slowly circling the plinths. "The preserver was a true artist."

"He was a friend of the old master's," I said, glancing at Donald. "We've found papers. The third plinth must contain more."

Fairchild looked up. "I brought a few tools."

I tapped the locked drawer. "We promise not to complain about any scratches."

"Scratches?" She gave the word such chilling hauteur, as if the mere implication were an insult; all the others laughed.

"After tea," I suggested. "The rest of you can start telling us what to do with the land."

"We haven't even seen it yet," Sunnam protested. "And I for one will have nothing useful to say."

Elizabeth patted his arm. "That's *never* true. Besides, we've had all those letters."

I started pouring, passing around cups, listening. They all talked over each other, as I'd very much expected. Where else in England, I thought, are there gatherings like this? We can't have been the only such group of friends. I caught Donald's eye; he smiled at me; then his attention was pulled back to the debate.

"But the apple trees. How many acres? The cider house – what about distilling? You remember that unearthly apple brandy in Normandy – a license? Well, that's what lawyers are for – how much land altogether? What about the dairy? Oh, you have Jerseys? What are those sheep good for? – a model farm – the landscape is so pretty – three good-sized towns so close – a cottage?"

"Wait!" Everyone sat up straight and stared at Elizabeth. She looked so excited. "I used to go with my grandfather to Rockaway, it's not far from Manhattan, in the summer. There were bungalows there, a little colony called Arverne. Artists and theater people would go on retreat anywhere they could in the summer, the city was a misery, but this place was full of, well," she produced a dismissive half-shrug that we knew meant 'people with money.' Then she sat forward. "I talked to *so many people* in London who wanted to get out of the city. For months or weeks or even a few days. They talked about the Lake District and the Cotswolds. Why not here?"

Donald and I blinked at each other. "There are no cottages," he said, but not in a way that meant 'and therefore this idea is a non-starter.'

"We could build cottages," I said; it might've been a question. "We'd need an investor."

Elizabeth happily cried, "What a coincidence!"

Instantly we tumbled into another gabble of discussion. "Should they look new? No, the whole idea is to enjoy the old-fashioned country. Stone walls – thatched roofs? Oh, and what about plumbing? – how far from the main house? you don't want a maze of roads – not too fancy. No daily service, not for a retreat – maybe an afternoon reception in the garden? You don't want people tramping through your house."

Fairchild effectively ended the discussion by setting aside her saucer. "We should return to this tomorrow evening, once we've been over the land. It sounds an excellent notion to me. You'll want to consult various authorities without delay, to see about land use, licenses, and the like." She gave Donald a steady look. "Retain counsel, sir."

"I will!"

"And if any land adjoining yours is available, you may wish to acquire it before any work goes forward."

Donald and I stared at each other, half-panicked. We both knew of such holiday colonies; we'd even stayed at them, though not together. Only the fact that such a wealth of intellectual resource was available to us kept us from immediately rejecting the idea of building. Well, that and the very high probability that we wouldn't plunge into debt. Elizabeth et al. would never permit that. And I knew with Marius involved, every cent of investment would be scrutinized. "Yes," I said, after a moment. "My goodness. I shall look at the cider house with completely fresh eyes tomorrow."

"And speaking of fresh eyes," Elizabeth said, getting to her feet. "Fairchild?"

The Duchess took a hand out of her trouser pocket, dangling a ring of shiny, spiky metal things. Then she bent to the drawer beneath the blue dragon. We all watched intently, though we could see nothing of what she did. We could only hear her swearing. "Buggering bitching bastard." Elizabeth started giggling, but she composed herself as the suspense drew out. We listened to the faint clink of metal against metal, and more swearing. At least two of us were in a fever of anxious anticipation. Finally, "Aha! Got you, you blighter." Fairchild stood back, straightened her spine, rolled her shoulders.

"Put up a fight, did it?" Elizabeth slipped an arm around Fairchild's waist and pushed up on tiptoes to kiss her cheek. "Aurelia, will you do the honors?"

I was already on my feet. What would we find? The delicate pull was between my fingers; I tugged gently and the drawer slid free. Inside was the key, along with a litter of gemstones. I felt breath on my face; turned my head to smile at Donald. “Look. Turquoise? Lapis? He did like to match his colors.” Many I did not recognize; some seemed mere pebbles. I scuffled through to an underlying sheet of paper describing the blue dragon. It was written, same as the others, in a clear hand that must have belonged to the preserver. I read it out to the others. “Blue phase white-lipped viper with bat wings paved with blue morpho wings, crest a dorsal fin, feet from gallinules. What’s a gallinule?”

“It’s a marsh bird,” Fairchild said. “Moor hen, brightly colored, walks on lily pads.”

Donald picked up one of the polished stones and carried it over to a lamp. “Look at this, darling. What is it?”

Elizabeth followed me over. I gave her a look meant to convey ignorance; she smiled. “It *might* be a sapphire,” she said. “Mr. LaSalle would know. That color, between sky and ocean, and the chatoyance.”

“What’s that?” said several people.

“The cat’s eye effect,” she mused. “But this one has schiller as well.”

The same people said, “What’s that?”

She took Donald’s hand and moved it. “You see the iridescence, when you turn it to the light?”

“We could call it dragon’s eye,” Donald said to me. “It nearly matches yours.” He bent and kissed me, right there in front of everyone. I had to blink back tears when he straightened up, muttering about a necklace, apparently unconscious of laying claim to me.

Elizabeth had her arm around my waist now, giving me a squeeze.

She led me over to the settee near the fireplace, unlit because the day was warm. With so many people in the room, and so many lamps, none of us had missed it. Now I thought about the coming winter, when perhaps we would be planning in earnest to begin a great work on our land. Our own village of cottages to fill with city folk on holiday, artists and bankers and lawyers. Maybe the same people would come year after year, becoming a family to us along with the people in this room. I blew out a breath.

Elizabeth handed me a fresh cup of tea. "Oh thank you, pet," I said. "I'm meant to be the hostess here."

"For heaven's sake." We both laughed softly. "It's not every day you uncover a third of a dragon hoard in your house."

"I should open the cabinet below. We've found some very interesting papers."

"Time enough for that tomorrow," she said. "You and Donald seem very content."

"Oh, Lizzie, we're so far beyond content. It's hard to believe we met through the newspaper."

She spoke very low. "Donald is very well-suited to being a husband, and if I wanted such a thing he'd never have needed to place an advertisement. But I'm not made for one man. One person." We made eye contact, both smiling a little. "I'm truly happy that he found you."

"And I," I said deliberately, "am truly happy that he found *you*." She leaned over, quick as a cat, and gave me a light kiss. Then we settled back to listen to the new discussion, which seemed to revolve around distilling. "A drop of apple brandy wouldn't go amiss," I said after a while.

"I visited a distiller in Scotland last year," Elizabeth said, eyes wide. "The smell of it! Astonishing!" I asked her about that, and before long the others caught on, and then Donald went looking for our decanter of Scotch. It was a lovely night.

Donald

Midway through the Great Visitation (as Aurelia and I had taken to calling it), she and the others left me to my own devices while they went in teams to Birmingham and Leicester for preliminary inquiries into building and supplying the proposed cottages. The past days had been so full of activity, I was in truth quite relieved to be left to myself for a night.

At least I was until I realized that meant I was sleeping alone.

I lounged in bed for half an hour, trying to read The Origin of Species, before abruptly remembering the manuscript. We'd found it at the bottom of the cabinet under the blue dragon, bound up in string that looked to've been re-knotted many times.

Five minutes later, I was back in bed with the manuscript beside me. Even the usual methodical plod of travelogue would be an improvement over lying awake thinking of my friends abroad, happily sharing whichever beds, while I huddled alone in mine. In fact, I should hope for a plod: it would put me to sleep.

I was regretting my decision by midnight, as I squinted at the pages. Even more so three (possibly four) hours later, when I sobbed aloud.

His only words today:

Don't grieve so. We'll meet again.

I held him through the night, afraid to sleep lest I miss another word.

Toward dawn, so softly that had not my every cell been listening I could not have heard:

Every day was joy.

I held him yet hours longer, imagining I felt even one more breath.

xx

It is over.

My life is over.

My love is gone.

xx

I do not know how long I sat at the table with his preserver's tools before me. Tempted by the knives, and the arsenic.

Our housekeeper took the case from my hands.

xx

His new creature comes back with me to England, its wings and talons carefully bestowed in straw. I leave my wings, and my heart, in Africa.

xx

I read this over every year or so. Not on any particular day, since we had no specific remembrances – my life began when we met, but neither of us could recall the exact day or time – but when I find myself craving his touch, his voice, to the point of pain.

Every time, I think: it should be published, only because otherwise, after me, he may be entirely forgot. Even my mother, who knew about us, did not truly understand.

Too much scandal. Too much risk.

Perhaps this will come to light someday, in a distant future when our five-and-forty years of love may be celebrated rather than condemned.

I will leave it with the other things. To whomever finally reads this: if you believe only five words of this fantastical tale, believe these:

it was a true love.

"Oh God," I muttered some time later, having soaked through my handkerchief and still sniffling. Pulled back the bedcurtains, shuffled my feet into slippers, tottered to the window like an old man. Peeked through the draperies: it was near dawn. Utterly no point in trying to sleep. I straightened my pyjamas, then wrapped myself in the old-fashioned dressing gown Mrs. Morris had excavated from a trunk, took myself to the washroom, and crept downstairs. Made myself a pot of tea (the desirability of a cookstove cannot be overstated) and sat at the kitchen table. A few minutes later Cook's cat found me. We regarded each other for a moment; I uncrossed my legs; it jumped up to my lap. Turned around twice, pummeled me a bit, then subsided into a warm, purring knot. I tentatively laid a hand on it, then stroked it; there was no objection. I was, if not consoled, at least comforted.

Cook joined me there not long after. She observed the situation, brought the kettle to warm my cup, then began her day. I watched her stoke the fire, bring proofed dough from a cupboard, and commence the morning's bread. I felt at home. The household staff were all used to me – to us – now. We were not the nose-in-the-air toffs, or aspiring toffs, they'd half-expected. I stroked the cat again, smiling to myself. Smiling my thanks when Cook brought me a dish of porridge with stewed apples and cream.

The others arrived home around midday. A hearty luncheon, then a long ramble as we talked over everything they'd learned; tea in the reception room, and some music. Then I told them about the manuscript.

Fairchild stared at nothing for a while before shaking her head and turning to me. "I'm bloody glad you were the ones to find it. Others might've pitched it on the fire."

No doubt she was thinking of her own Freddy, and his long love affair with Inigo Salazar. How lucky the Duke had been to find her. I said none of that. "There's no country on earth where he could have published, is there?"

Everyone shook their heads, evincing moods from resignation to glumness. Aurelia said, "To publish it, he'd've had to erase the story of their love. Of course he couldn't face that. But we could. I'd take it on. Keep the true story for some later day, but for now … at least the world could know what remarkable men they were. Their life of adventure could still be shared."

We'd found a single photograph of the two men together, in trekking gear, one with his arm slung over the other's shoulders, both smiling at the camera. "That picture of them in the mountains."

She nodded. "A wonderful frontispiece. And all of those drawings."

Then the discussion turned, as ours always did. This time to the gemstones and other artifacts; the possibility of keeping some for a private museum (a proposed attraction for the cottages) and auctioning others; whether the memoir should be published first. Such inexpressible joy, to have so many possibilities.

A few days more, and we were alone again. Thoroughly settled into our home now, a bright future ahead, and the bedroom door securely locked. I didn't quite realize that I was humming – I was in a pleasantly trancelike state – until Aurelia began to giggle. Then I heard myself. Consulted my various parts, one of which was in a state of high excitement, two of which were bound to the bedposts with silken cords formerly employed by the draperies. Arched my back, wriggled suggestively, and sang, "To rescue such a one as I from his unfortunate position."

Aurelia laughed out loud, then leaned down to sing softly against my mouth, "No no, not one!"

"For shame, darling." My voice was husky.

"Take any heart – take mine." She kissed me softly, lingeringly, lovingly. Her heart in her eyes.

And my own heart bloomed with a perhaps-belated realization. "My dear, is it possible we're in love?"

THE END

Of

The Blue Dragon

Read on for

THE SCARLET KNIFE

Severin

I was pleased to meet the dowager Duchess of --, that summer of 1905, mostly because I craved the acquaintance of anyone likely to ease my sense of alienation. George Fairchild had, at least, been to India. She knew my English family. She was notoriously free-thinking. And, having now met Elizabeth Bonner (known to be, of late, a bosom friend to the Duchess), I could not help suspecting that free-thinking meant everything I wished it would.

The laws of England and the laws of my home country do not notably differ on some points. However, in my own home, on my own land, I was accustomed to certain freedoms which I was loath to test on the sceptered isle.

In short, I was desperate for a fuck and likely to remain so. As usual, I sublimated my discomfort, saw to myself in private, and counted the days till I might return home. The Duchess had suggested I remove from London to Oxford. The Equatorial Club, where I was lodging, furnished private withdrawing rooms that I suspected could have been put to my use in perfect safety. But the cousin of a Marquess cannot afford to make assumptions. And there was so very much business to be undertaken.

An invitation to dinner with Miss Bonner (specifying 'to join a party of my Oxford friends') was extremely welcome. That it led, shortly after, to an invitation from the Duchess (everyone still called her that, even though her husband's brother had long since taken the title, and his wife was known to be annoyed by the existence of a dowager Duchess younger than the actual) to tea. There were few households more likely to provide congenial company, so of course I accepted.

Miss Bonner must also have been invited on this occasion, and must have learned that I was; in any case, she sent in a card on the afternoon in question, offering a seat in her conveyance. When I walked out, her driver tapped the brim of his hat with his whip; a sturdy terrier perched beside him cocked its head and offered a friendly yip; and Miss Bonner said, "Mr. LaSalle! You are so prompt!"

I bowed. "I am much obliged, madam, and wished not to keep you waiting."

"Which I very much appreciate, because if I hadn't wanted to have you to myself for a bit of conversation, I would have been riding. Come up." She budged over, gathering her skirts to make room.

I clambered up into the smart Victoria carriage, taking my seat along with a moment to appreciate her ensemble. The woman dressed superbly. She offered a gloved hand; I dropped a kiss on the back of it, then braced my feet against the front of the compartment, and we were off. "May I be of service in some manner?"

She gave me a warm look. "You may have grasped that my residence in England owes much to my wish to continue my education, more or less unto infinity, though I confess the calculus is very far down my list." She allowed time for me to laugh, waved off my apology, then went on. "I suppose, as an engineer, you are well acquainted with mathematics?"

"We are friends," I said, smiling. "My sister is the more naturally gifted."

"Oh! Did she go to college too?"

"No, but I taught her everything I could. We have reason to expect it will be her children, not mine, to carry on the business; and her intellect is second to none."

"I *knew* I liked you. Well, to get to the point, after our conversation the night we met, I acquired the books you mentioned. I've become completely fascinated with the science of gemstones, and I wondered if you might spare me time to answer questions?"

"I'd be delighted," I said sincerely. "It is the only subject in which I may claim to be an expert."

"Whereas my knowledge at this time goes no farther than ooh, sparkly." She watched with satisfaction as I laughed again. Then she asked a leading question. We were talking about the especial challenge of identifying red gemstones when the carriage pulled up.

The great doors swung open; a remarkable butler made us welcome. We were barely over the threshold when the Duchess appeared at the far side of the entrance hall and said, "Ah, there you are. Come and see the new nest in the conservatory."

Miss Bonner bounced across the hall, offering a hand. I would swear if I were not there, they would have kissed. It was delightful. She was saying, "Ooh! What kind of nest?"

"A blue tit, in one of my orange trees." The Duchess led the way.

Having appreciated the nest and left its bright-eyed tenant to her business, we returned to the library, where the Duchess clearly spent much of her time. She rang for tea, saying something to her servant that I entirely failed to catch. A few minutes later, someone joined us, and I nearly emitted a wholly improper epithet. The man was … well, he was the living embodiment of my ideal. Did I then, under cover of civil greetings, curse my luck that I had not met him decades before? Of course. He was at least my age, nearly my height, slim and sloe-eyed with graying black hair not unlike mine.

"You're lodging at the Equatorial?"

His question surprised me, but I nodded. "I much prefer a club to a common inn, and was recommended the Equatorial by a new friend in London."

"I've told Inigo about you, Mr. LaSalle," the Duchess said casually. "He dines there regularly. You have interests in common."

Do we, I thought, eyeing him. Before I could venture upon my usual topics – gemstones and the Empire – he spoke again. "Alfred, the late Duke, was a dear friend of mine. He left me something I've never had properly valued. I know you are not a jeweler, and I don't wish to give offense, but perhaps?" He let that trail off suggestively.

"Oh, I'm never happier than with my loupe in hand," I boldly lied. At least I had it with me; it was as much part of my daily attire as my pocket watch. "If you'd like me to see something?" I let *that* trail off suggestively.

"Perhaps you might join me in my study?"

"Of course. Your grace, Miss Bonner, you will excuse me?"

"Naturally." Oh, such subtle amusement in that smooth tone. The Duchess glanced at Miss Bonner, who instantly waved us away, saying something about wanting a private word with Fairchild.

A private *word*. I suspected that speaking together was the least of what they wanted. Calling the Duchess by her surname like that! As if they were fellows at college! I didn't know if I should be scandalized, or falling about laughing. In any case, I followed Señor Salazar meekly out of the room, down a hall, up a flight of stairs, and into a perfectly lovely room. It really was a study, not a bedroom, furnished much as the library downstairs with a desk, two reading chairs, a chaise longue, a fireplace, and gas lamps. "We still burn oil lamps at my estate," I remarked as he closed the door behind us. "Very likely will unto the mid-century."

"The Duchess follows the progress of electric systems with interest," he said, smiling. "So far, the generating plant required is too large and unsightly for her taste."

"We could talk about power sources and domestic aesthetics all day." We stared at each other for a moment. "Or we could discuss why you dine at the Equatorial."

He considered that for a few seconds. Considered me, and the way I was standing: weight on one leg, hands in my trouser pockets, unbuttoned jacket framing my hips. "I dine there with one or another trusted friend with whom I can … relax."

His accent was slightly sibilant. I shifted weight toward him. "How long have you lived in England, may I ask?"

"I came here with Alfred, more than twenty years ago."

"Then you knew him before he married!"

"Mmm. I was his … secretary." He took a step toward me. "And I've missed him terribly, the past five years."

Secretary, my arse. Well, he might've done that job in addition to the other. Though from the look of him, it had been a labor of love. "I had a dear friend back home," I offered. "He went down with his ship in a cyclone."

"We none of us reach any great age without loss."

Had he moved again, or had I? We stood very close together now. I very softly asked, "Did you lock that door?" He nodded, and I seized him.

Quite some time later, our hair and clothing restored to respectability and a window opened to freshen the room, Inigo unlocked the door and rang for coffee. Then he went to a box on the desk and lifted the lid. "I truly did mean to show you something," he said, with a trace of a smile. Oh, the man was beautiful, there was no other word. Mouth somewhat reddened from our kisses, eyes slumbrous from the rest. I was sprawled in one of the chairs; everything between knees and chest still trembled and ached. But I saw the glint of metal and the gleam of gemstones, so I heaved myself to my feet and joined him. "Blazing hell, where did he come by that?!"

"India." Inigo touched the knife. "I was there with him and the Duchess. They said this was inspired by a serpent called a kukri."

"Of course." I fished in my pocket for my loupe. Bent over the desk, heard a half-laughing intake of breath from Inigo, and shot him an amused glance. "Next time. Good Lord." The knife had an angled blade, common in South Asia, of highly-polished bronze. Nearly eight inches long, making it a proper weapon; but clearly a ceremonial piece. The handle was as long as the blade and entirely paved with small cabochon gems, mimicking the scales of a snake. Wide bands of scarlet, divided by thin rows of black, yellow, and black, set in bright gold. "Hmm." The black and yellow were almost certainly sapphires; the red might be spinel, rubies or garnets. On the butt was set a cloudy-green emerald carved with a snake. "A museum-quality piece. Or crown jewel."

"He said it would help fund a comfortable old age, should the need arise." He touched a band of yellow stones, then met my gaze as I straightened. "But the Duchess kept me on."

"She's obviously very fond of you."

"And I did not wish to go home to Madrid."

"Would anything tempt you from England?" We stared at each other for another silent moment. Then there was a tap at the door, and a servant entered with the coffee. It was too soon to pursue that conversation, thus a timely interruption. But I dearly hoped that we would speak of such things again. Among other things. Soon. Behind a locked door.

In the meantime, there was coffee, and the opportunity for private conversation with a man of unequalled allure. Inigo placed the bejeweled artifact back in its box, and came to sit with me.

Inigo

When we returned to the library, we found the Duchess alone. She graciously made no mention of the time elapsed, merely inquiring as to the scarlet knife. Mr. LaSalle asked her a number of questions regarding its provenance, some of which she was able to answer. He then summarized what he'd told me upstairs. "South Asian, ceremonial in nature, and almost certainly made for one or another of the maharajas, likely as part of a dowry or other political gift."

She sighed a little. “Freddy did inquire, but the seller could not prove, or perhaps was simply unwilling to identify, the original owner. I suppose it was stolen.”

“A great many artifacts have been taken by force from noble houses in India.” LaSalle’s tone was neutral; it was not an accusation.

“Should I sell it?” My interjection seemed to surprise both of them. I produced half a smile. “Were this a story in The Strand, I would fear a vengeful heir seeking to restore his patrimony, by fair means or foul.”

LaSalle reached over, grasped my forearm, and gave it a comforting squeeze; then sat back and said, “I doubt you’ve anything so sensational to fear, but there may come a time when your memory of the giver no longer inheres in the gift. At such a time, converting it into another sort of property may appeal. I am at your service, now or in the future, should you desire assistance in arranging a sale.”

“That reminds me,” Fairchild said, as Miss Bonner re-entered the room. “Lizzie, were you quite serious about your study of gemology?”

Miss Bonner sat, giving the Duchess a sideways look as she fluffed her skirts. “As you well know, I am *always* serious about *all* my studies.”

“Ah, of course. I beg your pardon,” in a sardonic murmur. Miss Bonner and I both stifled laughter; LaSalle gave me an amused look. Fairchild narrowed her eyes at me before turning to say, “Mr. LaSalle –”

“Severin, I beg you, your grace.”

She inclined her head. “Severin. Do call me Fairchild. I had half-promised Miss Bonner an afternoon’s fossick through my jewel case. A proper inventory and valuation are long overdue.”

What she meant was that certain things in her collection might be handed over to the current Duke and Duchess, painlessly greasing the family wheels. Fairchild still wore her wedding ring (now on her right hand) but was rarely seen with any other jewels beyond a fine pocket watch and a gold-cased compass, both formerly Freddy's. She did not look at me when she added, "If you would find such an afternoon entertaining, rather than an offensive imposition, your company would be enjoyable and your opinions valued."

LaSalle was leaning back in his chair, gaze traveling from one to another of us, brain almost visibly working. He was being invited to a quite intimate activity. Whether this was something Fairchild and Lizzie had cooked up between them while we were out of the room, or some new scheme, I could not guess; he must be even more at sea. I ventured, "Would I be present, your grace?"

"Heavens, yes, Inigo. You don't suppose I intend to sit with pen in hand? No, I shall sit idly by, telling stories of how each thing landed in my case, if I should happen to remember. Your assistance with the inventory is indispensable."

Ah. It was another excuse for me to spend time with LaSalle. Was I so very transparent? Well, no doubt I was; she had, after all, seen me with Freddy for nine of our twenty-two years. "I am, of course, at your service," I murmured.

LaSalle said, "As am I." He looked even more distinctly amused.

"Who knows," Fairchild said briskly. "I may decide to convert some of those glittering trifles into more useful forms of property. A new horse, perhaps."

"Or one of the new jalousie windows," Miss Bonner suggested, "to replace that rusted casement in your conservatory."

"Oh, excellent thought!" They were off on a discussion of recent innovations from America. LaSalle and I sat, contributing here and there, trying not to be too obvious about eyeing each other. I couldn't wait to be alone with him again.

Of course, Fairchild saw everything. When we were alone, celebrating a fine evening by having our dinner on the terrace outside the dining room, she said, "If you were a gas jet, he would be the spark, wouldn't he?"

I leaned my head on my hand, laughing helplessly. After a moment to overcome the embarrassment, I straightened and cleared my throat. "When you mentioned him before, you gave no hint."

She looked pleased. "No, I didn't, did I?"

"You said, I met an interesting colonial, he runs a sapphire mine in Ceylon that belongs to the Marquess of Rowland. All the ladies in town wonder why he's unmarried and speculate that he has a native concubine, or a harem. Did you deliberately obscure the issue?"

"Not deliberately," she hedged. Then she reached over, exactly as LaSalle had done, to grasp and squeeze my forearm. "My dear sir. He is nothing like Freddy, and yet I thought at once that they would have liked each other tremendously. The immediately-following thought was that you would like him too. Had we ever gone to Ceylon, we might all have met before."

I twitched, a sort of involuntary full-body expression of discomfort. What if we *had* all met? Freddy and I never strayed from each other, but with LaSalle's striking looks and quick-witted vigor before us, what might have befallen? I searched for a path away from that. "He is my junior by five years. When we were in India, he might have seemed too young." She made a dismissive sound, justifiably, since we both knew age had little to do with attraction. Or with one's ability to form a deep and lasting bond. I gazed at her for a long moment. "If we should grow close, will you mind?"

"Señor Salazar, how dare you imply I would be so selfishly possessive. I who have the world at my feet."

And Miss Bonner in Oxford, I thought and did not say. But her tone was distinctly injured, so, "Forgive me, your grace."

Now an impatient sound. "Devil take it, Inigo. Have I not said, repeatedly, that I feared your life had become a mere shadow? You may have yet forty years in your dish. Why should you not spend them in company with someone who can truly meet your needs? I know I am your friend. I love you like, well, an uncle." She grimaced, and I softly laughed. She was leaning forward, elbows on the table, wineglass held in both her hands, smiling ruefully. "An older brother, perhaps. In any case I cannot be all for you, any more than I could be all for Freddy. I liked LaSalle for you, and I like him with you. You'll see him again?"

I could make, in honesty, only one answer. "As soon and as often as possible."

The jewelry inventory may have been a whim, but Fairchild, as usual, followed through. It made for an extremely entertaining afternoon, leading into dinner with LaSalle and Miss Bonner, after which I invited LaSalle to my study for coffee and conversation. The Duchess made no reference, the following day, to what form that conversation may have taken; nor to the fact that LaSalle took his breakfast with me.

I offered no explanations, then or later, for my suddenly more frequent rides into Oxford. If I occasionally undertook an errand in town which would ordinarily have been executed by another, no one saw fit to comment. If I occasionally rode out before noon and did not return until after dark, it went unremarked.

He became our frequent guest for afternoon tea or for dinner. Had either of us been a woman, one would have said that we were courting. We spoke at length about our present lives: the daily routines, the social engagements, the friends we had in England and abroad. We also spoke of our past lives. We had both enjoyed considerable freedom in our youth; in his case, due to his peripatetic colonial upbringing; in mine, due to my position in my family. (My older brothers had been subject to higher expectations and greater control.) We were both on good terms with our families. We were both, by most measures, free to do what we would.

Other topics, such as the future, we left alone. One day, I knew, we would have to look each other in the eye and ask what came next. If it were even possible, for men who lived on opposite sides of the globe, to have a 'next.' For now, we seized the day.

It was clear to me, almost immediately, that my feelings for LaSalle were equal to my feelings for the late Duke. Surprising, and at times almost alarming: I had not imagined that a man of my age could feel so strongly at all, let alone so quickly. Had I ever believed that I would not (or could not) love again, I'd've been proven wrong. I will confess I'd wondered: would I, could I, if the odds should so favor me as to bring another such man to my door while I was still of an age to act on my attraction. Clearly the answer, to nearly everything, was Yes.

As you might imagine, after a few weeks of this, the question of what came next loomed large.

Severin

I did not expect this.

Had not sought it, could not have planned for it, and did not know what to do with it. The chances of meeting my ideal had always been vanishingly small; I'd repeatedly accepted a mere fraction of that ideal. Once faced with the man in full, I was thrown into deep confusion.

The truth was, I'd intended to stay no more than a year in England. I had never been here before; this was to be my one experience of it. A chance to meet all my relations; negotiate certain changes respecting the Ceylon property and the mine; see in person all the living history. After which, I'd expected to take ship home again and gradually work my way out of a controlling position. Become, at some not too far distant point, a gentleman of leisure. An advisor, perhaps; the person to whom the new management would come for suggestions on how to approach a new vein, or redirect the company as the world changed around us. I had expected, you understand, to live out my life essentially alone. No law will prevent men of like minds from finding each other, and I knew where to look. But someone to live with, to grow old with, to love? That was never in sight.

Except now it was, because I'd seen him. We'd held and tasted and reveled in each other. He'd seen all my scars, from the palimpsest left on my hands and arms by years in the gem gravel to the snakebite-withered hollow of my shin. I'd heard of his stifled youth and of his unimaginable freedom with his Duke. We'd talked for hours, discovering all the ways our views and wishes aligned. I did not want to give him up.

There came an evening when Inigo was otherwise engaged, and I – not caring to dine alone – invited myself to dinner with Miss Bonner. Her steward and tutor both being habitués of the Equatorial Club, this was easily accomplished. I then threw discretion to the four winds and laid the problem before them all.

"Here is the scenario," I said, after tossing back half a glass of fine Burgundy. "When I came to England I fully intended to return to Ceylon, in more or less the same condition as I left it, once I'd achieved my aims here. I have now a reason not to return at all, except that England provides me less freedom than I'm accustomed to. Less than I believe I could live with."

Miss Bonner, Marius, and Sunnam all blinked at me. I waited for one of them to speak. Raised my eyebrows at the young lady, who nodded as if I'd confirmed something and said, "Has this to do with a particular person, and a wish to spend the latter half of your lives together?"

"Precisely."

Marius and Sunnam looked at each other, then back at me. Marius said, "Have you thought about France?"

Now I blinked at him. "I had not."

"Different law there, you see." He explained it to me, briefly, no doubt aware that excitement would interfere with my comprehension (or patience). After winding up the thread, he added, "Sunnam and I have, well, Lizzie. This house is freedom and safety for us." He gave their young lady a warm look.

She blew him a kiss, saying, "I need you both, full stop, so you'll always have a home with me. But Severin – may I call you Severin?"

"Please."

"And you must call me Elizabeth, or Lizzie, depending on the mood. Are you saying you meant to go home next year after," she waved her hand; there was really no need to be specific. "But you don't have to?"

"If the Marquess agrees to take certain actions, I don't have to go back. My share from the mine has been accumulating for thirty years."

"Thirty!"

I smiled. "Well, I first put my hands in the sluice when I was five, but I took an active role in the company at fifteen."

"Gracious! So you could afford a house, perhaps in France, if you had a reason to establish yourself there."

"I could. If." I stopped myself while it was still possible to deny I had Inigo in mind. "Thank you for the suggestion. I had best arrange a trip to Yorkshire. I'm overdue, in any case." I had, to be honest, delayed opening the subject with my cousin simply because I didn't wish to leave Inigo.

Lizzie then changed the subject, mentioning a Yorkish expedition of her own, and at length I took myself off. In my room at the club, I debated speaking with Inigo. Telling him what changes were possible, what I'd meant to seek, and what I might add to that. Part of me wished to present him with a fait accompli; the more cautious part told me we should speak plainly before I made any irreversible decisions. We had so resolutely avoided speaking of the future. But every week that passed was a week closer to the time he expected me to depart. Why should I leave us both in suspense? So I wrote a brief note asking if I could call on him the next day; dispatched it by messenger; then put myself to bed with a weighty scientific journal, hoping it would send me to sleep.

Given my perturbed state of mind, imagine my feelings when Inigo replied with regrets; he was unable to meet for approximately a week, owing to his duties. He and the Duchess were away to London.

I used the time constructively, writing a detailed letter to my cousin the Marquess and following it with a wire. A few days later he replied with an invitation to stay at Rowland, in Yorkshire, from the first week of December until after Twelfth Night. I was given to understand that many of my cousins would also be there, at least part of the time. Some I had previously met, during my weeks in London. Others would be new acquaintances. With my proposed stay encompassing the Christmas holiday – which, in Ceylon, I did not celebrate – I immediately fell to worrying whether I should be prepared to distribute gifts of some kind.

When I put the question to Elizabeth, she heaved a sympathetic sigh. "I used to dread Christmas because the house would be full of people who I only saw once a year, all of them would expect something, and they'd have spent the past year gossiping about me. One year I gave them all books by Horatio Alger." My expression was, evidently, mystified; she said, "He wrote about young men who rise from poverty to riches through virtuous acts. It turned into a huge argument about what constitutes virtue. Pointless, but entertaining."

"In other words, you put a fox among the geese just to hear the honking." She laughed. I smiled, took a sip of tea (her housekeeper made it Indian style, thank the gods), and said, "You don't dread it this year, I take it."

"Oh, no, I can't *wait*. The only people I have around me now are people I care about. People I *know*. Choosing gifts is going to be such fun. But in your case," she paused, tapping a buffed fingernail against the marquetry tabletop. "You don't even know how many will be there on the key dates? Then perhaps the answer is a single thing that any number of people could share."

I gave her an admiring look. "How clever you are. Tell me, then: if you were sequestered in a north-country house for weeks of winter, what would you most crave?"

"Oh, goodness. I suppose they have even less daylight than we have here, so it's cold *and* dark. The obvious answer is unspeakable." She said it with such a sly expression that I laughed. Then she said, "I presume that the Marquess already has a piano, a library, and a good supply of liquor. Some contribution to the winter feasts, then?"

We fell to discussing whether I should play up the non-English side of my heritage, deciding that since I would likely be considered quite exotic I might as well embrace it. Thus I took myself to London to secure the ingredients, including a box of spices, for a rice pilaf with dried fruit that was a staple at home. Everything would keep for the intervening weeks. Considering that this might serve dozens, a sizable trunk was required. I also (while pretending not to wish I might cross paths with Inigo) followed a chain of referrals to a purveyor of game boards, etc., where I obtained a pachisi set, several decks of cards and, on a whim, an American game called Race Around the World. I did not expect the warm feelings this excursion engendered; upon reflection, on the train back to Oxford, I realized that I had been 'acting English' since my arrival. Reminding myself of my roots was a comfort. If it did come to pass that I never returned to Ceylon, I should make a point of celebrating my heritage.

That led me to wondering if Inigo did. I knew that Spanish-style cuisine was often on the menu Chez la Duchesse; I knew that Inigo corresponded with his family, and with other friends in Spain; but I had not asked if he returned to Madrid with any regularity. Or if he wished to. Were we to set up housekeeping together (and what a disorienting thought that was!), I would like him to be as Spanish as he cared to be. I did not even know if he was religious.

And upon *that* thought, I fell to worrying again. Even a lapsed Catholic might question forming a connection with one like myself, who was never a Christian at all.

Inigo

Had Severin's request to meet come in the usual way – that is, delivered in daylight – I should have thought nothing of it. His missive arrived so late that the house was already locked up, and the messenger had to come round to the kitchen door; I was composed for bed when the footman knocked. And then, concerned by the apparent urgency of the request, I fell to worrying so that I hardly slept. Had his plans changed? Did he mean to return to Ceylon early? Even if it were simply to say he was leaving the Equatorial Club to take lodgings in London again, I would fear that meant an end to our affair.

I did not want it to end.

The questions that crowded my mind could none of them be put on paper. I tried to write my reply in such a way that he could discern my wish to see him again as soon as may be. But then I had much business, of the sort that requires one's full attention, and my time was not my own.

I did not resent it. I told myself I did not. I told myself that, in fact, if I did not wish to carry out this sort of duty all I need do was tell Fairchild. She would relieve me. She would house me to the end of my days even if I were bone idle. For those reasons I did not ask to be relieved. I merely carried out my brief, attended to the London side of the business she and Miss Bonner and Marius were engaged in, and waited for them to finish.

Miss Bonner went back to Oxford before us. I was envious. Fairchild noticed. "You could go too, you know," she told me. "I have to speak with Agatha and Catriona again to ensure the case is wound up, but nothing remains that only you could accomplish."

"Nothing we've done is anything only I could accomplish," I said, with perhaps too much of an edge to my tone. Hearing it, I immediately apologized. "I am pleased that you trust me with such business," I assured her. "It's only that I have personal concerns at the moment."

She set down her glass with almost a thump. "Are you well?"

"Very well, Duchess."

"Have you troubling news from Spain?"

"No."

"Is it Severin?"

I closed my eyes for a second, huffing out a half-smiling sigh. "He asked to speak with me, the night before we embarked on this. I had to put him off, and I am worried, because he sent to me so late."

"Inigo. Pack your traps and go home. I've no idea what might be on his mind, but go and discover it. I'll be home in a few days." She would hear no argument, and in truth I did not offer one. I was on the first morning train.

Upon arrival in Oxford, part of me wished to stop at the club and ask to see Severin there. Instead, I sent in a note to the effect that I was at his service that afternoon or evening. At the house, I methodically unpacked; bathed; forced down a light meal; and told myself I was being absurd. If the man meant to sever our connection, he could have said so in any one of several subtle ways. I had read his note a dozen times and found no such meaning (and, as you may infer, I was looking for it). There were countless subjects on which he might have wished to speak. It was purely the timing of the message that worried me so.

Then a new message was delivered, and worry turned to hope.

In the hour before he arrived, I sought to distract myself by organizing Fairchild's recent correspondence. There was a letter for me, from my sister-in-law in Seville; I set it aside, thinking I would like to see my nieces and nephews again; the eldest was now betrothed, the youngest on his way to university. Then I heard the slight commotion of an arrival and sat back, breathing deep to compose myself. Amon brought Severin to the library door, announced him in the usual way (that is, like visiting royalty; the pair of them had taken to each other), then bowed himself out.

"Mr. LaSalle," I said after a moment, rising.

"Señor Salazar."

"For God's sake, call me Inigo." He did in private, and we *were* private, if yet clothed and upright.

He smiled a little. "Inigo. You must call me Severin. At all times."

I half-laughed, shaking my head. "Shall we talk here? Or perhaps you'd like to see the grounds. It's a fine day." And out in the park there would be no one, even Amon, to see or hear.

"A walk," he said. "I've recently been in London and am reminded how I miss trees."

I wondered why he'd gone to the city, but said nothing more until we were outside, away from even the scrape of a gardener's spade. "You miss Ceylon?"

"In truth? I miss my sister, and the rest of the family. I miss the activity of the mine, the landscape, the wild things. And I could do with less wool about my person."

That made me laugh. He'd complained before about English clothing, necessitated by English weather. But he was here to speak of serious things, not the weather. "Your message worried me. I feared you had reconsidered our friendship." The slightest pause before the final word; I felt too exposed to use one more exact.

"In a sense I *have* reconsidered, but perhaps in a way opposite your meaning," he said. We had stopped walking. Still within sight of the house, with woods before us and meadow behind. The leaves whispered in a breeze; birds sang; somewhere far off, we heard sheep complaining at each other. "There is business I must transact with my cousin at Rowland. He's invited me for a month at midwinter. I mean to go, and initiate certain arrangements, but before I do I must know." He stopped abruptly, as if afraid to say the next words.

We were almost of a height; I had only to lift my chin to make eye contact; yet I felt as though he were on his knees, asking for my hand. "Even Freddy never looked at me thus." I sucked in a breath, a bit horrified that I spoke aloud.

"How?"

In for a penny. "As if his world would end if I pushed him away."

He looked around, confirming that no other person was near, then took my hand between his. "For most of my life I've imagined a solitary future. I thought I could bear it; I thought I had no choice. But there *is* a choice, and now that solitary future is beyond bearing. I have lived all my life as a sort of vassal, and I would have freedom. In every sense. I would have a home entirely my own, to share with whomever I choose. I dreamed of these things before, in the way a young man dreams of things he has never seen. Now I want them, because I have known you, and I can picture a different life."

We were touching only at the hand, though standing very close together. "What would you have us do?"

All he said was, "France." My eyes went wide; I knew immediately what he meant, if only because of the recent discussions about Fairchild's protégée Agatha Fletcher. Perhaps he saw my nascent excitement; as if to warn me off, he said, "You must know I'm not a Christian."

"Cielos, mi amor, can you suppose I care?" We stared at each other, wet-eyed, hands trembling, beginning to smile. "Back to the house," I said, almost roughly. We were almost inside before I realized I still gripped his hand.

I was of not much use to Fairchild in the next weeks. She and Miss Bonner made plans to convey Agatha and Catriona to Provence and see them settled at the farm owned by longtime friends of Freddy's. Fairchild did not even ask if I wanted to go along; they meant to be away no less than two weeks, and no doubt my affect was that of a man who didn't wish to be away at all. She promised to bring back full details on the nearby village, because she was no fool. We also talked briefly of a trip to Spain, so that I could renew my acquaintance with my ever-more-extended family. But then she was away, leaving me in possession of both the house and my liberty.

Needless to say, I took full advantage of both, inviting Severin to stay. A room was prepared for him, down the hall from mine, for appearance's sake. It was never occupied. Apart from daily walks or rides, and an hour or two in Fairchild's library (for me to give the day's correspondence my attention while Severin browsed her collection of books), we spent the time almost entirely in my rooms.

Being men of a certain age, our time was not spent entirely in bed. We talked at length of the adventure of the Emerald Boa, entertaining ourselves for most of an evening by pretending we would write it up for The Strand. Aside from that, Severin had brought with him a copy of the handwritten journal of his ancestor. He said, "I thought you might find this of interest. My life has been entirely bound to the interests of the estate and the mine, and both took their current form during the first Severin's tenure. In fact, he discovered the gem gravel when he installed an aqueduct."

"Was he also an engineer, then?"

"No, only a lonely man with an unquiet mind."

"Let me read it." I took the box of foolscap from his hand, flipping through the first few dozen pages. "What age had he when this began?"

"Not quite thirty. He lived fifty more years."

"Fifty more!" That was a great age for any wealthy European, never mind one banished to the half-tamed tropics.

Severin reclined on the pillows stacked against the headboard, pulling me against his chest. I rested in the circle of his arm and began to read.

From the journal of Severin LaSalle

September 1794.

I hope that I may never again take ship across the seas. Not even to return to England would I suffer that.

The house is larger than I expected. Ferns grow where the walls meet the rafters, and lizards climb the walls, and I must daily disencourage the wild sow who claims the courtyard. I have not felt cool or clean since I arrived here.

English clothing will not do.

xx

I have found a star-gazing rock.

It is high up the hill, with a steep face but a sloping back. When I lie atop it, on a clear night, the heavens are awash in stars. It is astounding.

Did I never look up, in England?

xx

The factor has brought me a servant. I expected it to be a woman, as most domestic work is done here by women; she looks barely in her teens. She is very silent, but he says she can understand and speak some English. So far I have heard from her only 'yes, sahib' and 'no, sahib.'

After showing her the room where the cooking and washing is to be done, and the small room adjacent which is to be hers, I took the factor aside to ask where he had found her.

He tells me she is the daughter of a dock clerk in Colombo and his servant, and that he bought her at the clerk's request when her mother died.

Bought her! I said. How is this?

He said that the indenture common for such servants amounts to slavery, and may be passed from owner to owner; with such young women, it is typically a license to use the creature for any purpose.

I knew of indentures in England and never inquired. I was so incurious then. I hope the terms are not so vile.

xx

The factor has been by, bringing a letter from my mother. She is settled now in India.

I wish I might see her.

At least, I can write.

xx

December 1794.

I write this at sometime past midnight – my watch has run down – by the oil lamp, having just returned to the house from my accustomed ramble.

I have met the god of the forest.

I did not believe the men, when they told me there was a tiger on the plantation. A tiger! They do not live on this island, I was told, by every white man I have met. And according to the native art of India depicting a giant striped cat, which I saw before leaving England, what I have seen was not a tiger, but a leopard.

I was on the path about a quarter mile below my star-gazing rock, and attending chiefly to my footing, as I have many times misstepped on this irregular thoroughfare, but never encountered a beast more fearsome than a porcupine. A movement ahead caught my eye and I looked up, stopping so suddenly that I very nearly overbalanced myself.

He stood there, not ten feet away, staring at me.

His head was held low, and his tail waved slowly, ending each sidewise movement with a definitive flick. His eyes gleamed, the color unclear in the dim moonlight. His coat was a pale fawn marked with rings of black. He appeared as long and as tall as a mastiff, with a tail the length again of his body.

Frozen in shock, I locked eyes with the beast for perhaps longer than I should, before slowly and cautiously backing away up the path. He issued a sort of snarling hiss, horrible fangs flashing, and stood his ground until I was a good thirty feet back.

Then, apparently content that I offered no threat, he gathered himself and with one leap mounted a dozen feet up into the nearest sizable tree. I lost view of him entirely a moment later, and was barely able to hear that he jumped again from tree to tree, going away from the path.

I do not know how long I stood there, or when I first thought to breathe again.

I will go back up the path in daylight to see if I can find his foot-marks.

I skimmed ahead, noting reference to an episode of fever, and to dealings with the factor. "It was a cinnamon plantation?"

"Mmm. Very profitable, at the time."

Twisting around to make eye contact, I asked, "Is it still like that? The jungle, the animals?"

"Oh yes. If men were to depart, nature would have the land back to herself within a year, and only the empty structures would tell the tale. Till the jungle pulled them down again."

Having lived all my life in lands long subjected to agriculture, I shivered at that. "No other trace?"

"None." He caressed my hair. "It is not a place for the man, or woman, who fears uncertainty."

I huffed out a breath and flicked to a new page. A word caught my eye, and I reversed to the beginning of the entry. "Adaptation." A glance at Severin. "You said you felt bound by the estate."

"Very much so. It's," he hesitated, then sighed. "The kind of chain that one feels a fool to complain of. My father, and no doubt his before him, kept this book to remind himself and his children of our good fortune. How many half-breed sons of Empire are handed near-complete control of a prosperous estate? There was never an edict from the Marquess. Not from any of them. That Severin the First did not simply lie on the veranda and drink himself to death is a credit to him."

"And an example to you. All of you."

"Precisely. He was, essentially, in prison. But he made the best of it, so how could we do less?" He must have seen my frown at the word 'prison.' A light touch on my hand, a light kiss on the side of my face. "Read on. Only a bit more, I think. Then you'll see the charge that was laid on us."

December 1795.

My first adaptation has been a success.

The house is located in a clearing well up into the hills. It is surrounded, however, by thick forest, and benefits little from the breezes off the ocean. Many days I have lain on the bench set on the wide porch, wearing nothing but drawers, hoping to catch even the slightest movement of the air; it is so hot and humid.

At length, weary of bewailing my fate (however silently, as I have no one to bewail except the girl, and I have yet too much pride to lament myself in the face of someone brought so low by life), I spent an afternoon in proper study of the topography. And I thought, if certain nearby trees should be cut, and others more distant reduced in height, I should have a clear line of sight to the gulf below; and where the eye may see, surely the wind may blow.

Accordingly I went down to the village, and spoke to the headman, with the help of the grocer there who speaks good English; and arranged to have a crew of men come with their tools. The men here often mount up into the trees for the many kinds of fruit, or to hunt the birds and animals that live there, and they professed confidence in their ability to do what I wished.

We began after the monsoon, and it has taken some time, as we have essayed the project in stages. A number of tall trees nearest the house were taken down. Then the crew attacked the more distant growth. (If this should ever be read by someone unfamiliar with Ceylon, mind you that our forest here bears little resemblance to a well-groomed English wood. For every thick-trunked tree, there are five or six, or a dozen, spindly neighbors. I am told these will seize their new advantage and instantly fill the vacated space unless beheaded - so we have done so.)

A first cut was found to be too high, et cetera, and I wished to avoid killing the trees, if possible, since they provide so much good to the human inhabitants of this plantation; not to mention the animals. I believe the men would have cut all the trees at the ground if I had not insisted on working from the top down.

I see that their lives are more regularly at odds with nature than mine, since I do not rely for my very food on the work of my own hands.

Moreover, they have no time to sit quietly and listen to the forest. I cannot expect that, to them, it is any more than an obstacle to be surmounted; whereas for me, the forest and the life therein are become my greatest comfort.

At any rate, the trees have been topped, the sunset now lights up my porch, and the sea breeze refreshes me.

xx

September 1796.

I see that the first pages of this journal have begun to disintegrate. The climate here is not kind to paper; all of the books I brought with me have perished. I have a supply now of less transient writing material, though little of which to write. Nevertheless, I have copied everything over. This journal will be the only proof I ever lived.

The great change, conveyed to me by the factor, is immaterial; no-one fights here, and whether Dutch or English hold the coast is a matter of indifference to me. I suppose he is more exercised since it is his task to arrange the shipping.

By my reckoning I have now been away from England for nearly thirty months. I rather wish my cousin had me hanged, instead of this.

xx

December 1796.

She called me by my name today. It is a stunning victory. Why do I care? Because she is kind, and has borne with me uncomplaining all these months? I think it is more than that.

Perhaps, having had her literally pry the means of my destruction from my hand, I have tendered my life to her. And so, for her to speak to me as another person, not just the white man that houses her; to hear my name, from another person … I felt like shouting with joy. If I had not thought I would frighten her, I might well have.

Once I was Sir Aubrey Delville, Bart., lord of a fine, if modest, manor in Dorset. I wonder if that Captain has called it other than Berry Hill? If he ever thinks of the fool who wagered it away?

Now I am lord only of this mossy house in the forest.

Now I am not master, sahib, sir, or even Mr. LaSalle. I am Severin. It is enough.

It was enough for one night. I sat up and leaned across Severin to drop the box on the bedside table. "So long, and still he lived chastely with her?"

"Until they married. More than three years in all." He laughed at my expression. "If you read it in full, you will see how he struggled with it. He was determined not to despoil her. Positive he should have no children."

"He believed his line should end with him," I translated. "What on earth had he done?"

So he told me the story, one of drink and gambling and reckless violence. The attempted assassination of his cousin, the then Marquess, resulting in the death of a different man. The family had dealt with it in law, but privately. "The drink took him yet twice more. Once not long after he married, and once years later when his mother died in India. My own father was the worse for drink, many times. There are some who say it is a hereditary weakness." Severin shrugged. "I have never been much tempted."

"You've lived a public life," I said, feeling my way. "Moving freely about the eastern colonies, going to college, representing the business. You had to keep your wits about you." That made him smile. I laid a hand on his chest, over his heart. "And you had no wife's hand on your tiller."

Now he laughed. "No, indeed. If I were to remain on course, I must manage it myself. The gods know my old friend was more apt to steer me onto shoals."

Suddenly I felt our own keel scraping the bottom. I should say nothing, or change the subject. Instead I heard myself say, "Did you love him?"

Severin turned to his side, wrapping an arm over me, nuzzling into the side of my neck. "Not as you loved your Freddy, but I cared for him. He was the person who knew me best. I knew from an early age that I should not marry. Should not make the pretense of it, which meant a life alone. That understanding," he paused, face still hidden from me. "I will not say he was the best I could do, because that, my dear, is you. But the best at that time: yes."

I got my hand under his chin and turned his face up to mine. We stared at each other in eloquent silence. An outside observer might believe it was too soon to say that he was the best for me, or I for him. But I had fallen once before, in just such a tumultuous, hasty, joyous rush; and not for a moment had I regretted it. I meant to say something. Instead I pressed my mouth to his, felt his strong arm wrap about me, and fell again.

Severin

For the purpose of this narrative, we may pass over the next several weeks. Suffice to say that Inigo and I, once the Duchess returned and I removed myself from her house, continued to see each other almost daily. Our friends provided safe haven. We spoke little about the future, but this time it was because until I finished my business in Yorkshire there was no point. We had already agreed that, whatever the result of that business, we meant to set up a household together in France. To live together, committed, as life partners. Thus when it was time for me to go North, Inigo was at the Equatorial Club to kiss me goodbye in private, and then at the train station to see me off.

It was a long journey, tedious and cold enough to make me deeply resent my solitude. I would like to say I filled the time constructively in reading or correspondence. In truth, I spent hours staring out the window thinking about the letter I'd sent my sister Helen the month before. She should have received it already. My intentions were not unknown to her, but she might well have thought I'd change my mind. She might have feared I'd return to Ceylon with an English wife, determined to play the conventional role. To betray her.

Well, she would know better soon. Once all was agreed, I would write again.

I was made lavishly welcome by everyone in the castle (my cousin did not call it that, but let us make no pretense), including the cook, who enthused over the spice-box and declared her willingness to essay the rice pilaf on whichever night saw the most guests. There were tours both inside and out, sleigh rides in the home wood, outings to the nearest town, stories from the family history. I was indeed an exotic novelty, but no one meant to give offense, and I took none.

It was near the end of the first week before I broached the subject of the property in Ceylon; I am not completely uncivilized, after all. The Marquess may have thought otherwise. He gave me the sort of look that highly-placed men have been wont to give those less highly placed since the notion of rank was first devised. I narrowed my eyes back at him. "Walter, it isn't mine. It never was. A nominal lease and a life interest are not the same as legal title, and you know it."

He sighed gustily and threw himself into the sturdy (if dog-gnawed) armchair across from me. "You're saying I should bestir myself as none of my predecessors have, and properly transfer the property."

"You should, but not to me."

Now he blinked at me with an expression of blank surprise. I held my tongue. After nearly a minute of silence, he said, "Please elucidate."

I took a moment to sip the excellent whisky in my glass, appreciating the way the cut crystal refracted the firelight. "I am not going to marry, Walter. There will be no heir through my line. I want you to give the property to my sister."

Another silence, then, "Not your nephew?"

"In time Helen will pass it on to whichever of her children she deems most able. But she has, today, all the same knowledge and connections I do. And – I don't know if you've ever taken note – four times out of five, investment in a man results in profit wasted on intoxicants, gambling, and whores." Walter barked out a laugh. I smiled at him. "Whereas four times out of five, investment in a woman results in an improved standard of living for everyone around her. Therefore, I suggest making the transfer without specifying male heirs."

He thought this over with his usual gravity. "You say you will not marry."

"I will not. Let us not, I pray, examine my reasons." He inclined his head. No doubt he'd heard of my resolute disinterest in all the Society ladies to whom I'd been eagerly introduced, and no doubt he'd drawn some conclusions. "There is something further." He raised his eyebrows, inviting me to speak on. "I contemplate relocation, specifically to France. Perhaps the company would benefit from having a representative in Europe."

"Hmm. So it would." He did not ask 'why France,' or 'why not England.' The answer to both was the same as the answer to why I would not marry. After a moment he sighed again, then picked up his glass and sipped his own whisky. "You've done extraordinary things with the mine."

"Thank you. The original seam is nearly played out, though, my lord. There may be more riches deeper inside the hill, but getting at them would destroy both the property and the lives of everything downstream. The gravel found in the new tract is more promising. Helen knows all about it. She is poised to begin construction as soon as you authorize it."

"Or as soon as my authorization is no longer required."

"As you say." We both sipped again, stretched our feet out to the fire again, thought our private thoughts again. I realized he was looking at me with a degree of fondness. Considering that till now we'd known each other only by letters and telegrams, it surprised me. "Have I in some way pleased you?"

"Oh, Severin, for the good Lord's sake. You've been an asset to the family since you could toddle. Your entire line has been. My great-grandsire never expected anything from yours. He'd've said that simply managing the cinnamon harvest without mishap was enough. To then have Severin the First fling gemstones at him – well, you should see his diary from that time. And the marginal commentary from his lady." Walter snickered into his glass. "In truth, to have you near enough for the occasional actual conversation would please me. No one is better qualified to represent us on the Continent. And I'm sure Helen is very well qualified to assume control from you. Will you return to Ceylon at all?"

I hadn't decided; that sort of planning had to wait upon the result of this conference. "Let us say, I may visit."

He nodded again. "Then you will remain in England for a time? Good. I'll initiate the transfer." We discussed the likely timeline for that process, and where I was likely to be at certain points on the timeline. By then our glasses were empty. Outside, the sky was still light; he suggested a stroll round the castle before we went to dress for dinner. I said nothing about my general lack of enthusiasm for outdoor activity in Yorkshire in December. My cousin was, much to my relief, a congenial companion; cementing this relationship was to my advantage in every way. And the boot room was full of coats heavier than anything I'd ever owned. As we walked, I told him about my wish to publish the first Severin's journal. He suggested that the English side of that story might be of interest. The letters were few, but carefully preserved by the Rowland archivist. Before long, our discussion was so animated that I almost forgot how beastly cold it was.

Inigo

Fairchild and I were dining à deux in her private study, as we often did during the winter; she always said there was no point heating the dining room when only two seats at the great table were occupied. Besides, this way the staff could set all ready for us, then retire to their own dinner in the cozy room adjoining the kitchen. It was an excellent rationale, and one I never questioned; I knew perfectly well that she preferred a simpler way of life. That she kept such a house at all was due primarily to Society's expectations of a Duchess (even a dowager). We'd moved on from soup to fish before she mentioned hearing from Mr. LaSalle.

I set down my fork and looked up. Oh, such an affectionate look. I cleared my throat. "I've heard from him as well."

"Have you?"

"He wrote from Yorkshire. Spending the month with his cousin, you know."

"The Marquess of Rowland," she said judiciously. "A pleasant, intelligent man; not a wastrel; kind to animals and loving with his wife. Had they met before?"

"Not in person. Years of correspondence, I take it."

"Wait, Inigo. Had *you* ever met the Marquess? This one, I mean?"

I shook my head. "You say he is pleasant."

"He was on the town during my Season. My parents threw me at him several times. We got on well enough, but." She shrugged, half-smiling. "Happily, he chose another." No need to say she was not the wife for a man who wanted children. Rowland already had four.

I ate the rest of my fish. Swallowed some of the Chablis in my glass. Thought about my letter from Severin. Waited for Fairchild to set down her fork. "He said he's asked Rowland to deed the Ceylon property to his sister."

Fairchild nearly choked on a mouthful of wine. "He's done *what*?"

"Told the man he won't marry, thus there will be no heir, and the best person to manage it going forward is his sister. Says he didn't precisely demand the deed, it was Rowland's suggestion. Severin," I caught myself. It was indiscreet to use his given name. But this was Fairchild, after all, and she was giving me a particular look. "He told Rowland that he means to relocate to France."

"Oh. I see." No doubt she did. We stared at each other for a few seconds, then busied ourselves with the fragrant Spanish-style chicken and rice in the next dish. I refilled our glasses. Eventually she said, "I suppose he wants you to relocate with him."

I sighed. There was no prevaricating. "He has said so."

A sharp look now. "I suppose you've had ample time for that kind of conversation, amongst all the others."

I sputtered out a laugh. "It was a relief. As have been the others."

Her turn to laugh. Then, "Hmm. France." Her gaze went unfocused, as that complicated mind went to work.

I left her to it. In truth, I could hardly imagine what kind of life Severin and I might have together. The only men I knew who shared my nature lived either alone, or as part of a large household. Miss Bonner's steward Marius had told me that he hoped Sunnam Gould would lodge with them after leaving Oxford; even that wasn't the same thing. I knew there were men who shared lodgings, privately. It simply wasn't spoken of. Ten years after Oscar Wilde was sent to prison, most of us were still too untrusting to speak outside of the few gathering places where we all shared the same risks. But in France … well, things could be different. I could never shed forty years' training in discretion, but at least we could not be arrested for what we did together behind closed doors.

Fairchild interrupted my thoughts. "We've spoken of the village where we settled Agatha and Catriona. Could you see yourself there?"

I blinked at her. It sounded a lovely place; not too remote, but not likely to be overrun, and we would already have acquaintance there. I wondered if she had some enterprise in mind. "What would we do?"

"Hell's teeth, Inigo, how should I know? I doubt the Marquess would willingly dispense with Severin's expertise, but he's a bloody engineer; he could do what he likes. You're capable of managing any kind of business. You could teach, as you once suggested. Or you could sit in the sun and grow tomatoes."

I laughed again. "Enjoy a life of leisure? More leisure than I have now?"

"I keep you busy enough," she grumbled. "I'd have the devil of a time finding a better secretary, let alone one who could tolerate my ways."

"Make off with Miss Bonner's tutor," I suggested. "I collect he has no intention of actually taking holy orders." She cackled, shaking her head, setting her glass down in the nick of time.

Severin

While I enjoyed my time in the North, I was not sorry to leave frigid Yorkshire and return to more temperate Oxford. New letters were on their way to Ceylon; my cousin's men-at-law had commenced drafting the transfer agreement; I had formally disavowed any intention of seeking reinstatement of my ancestor's long-vacated title. I had also established a degree of friendship with many of my relations, which I expected to stand me in good stead in the coming years.

Letters to Inigo preceded me. One per week, carefully crafted to appear part of an ongoing conversation between mere friends. Love letters had brought down enough men of our sort, and while the members of Fairchild's household would not betray us, the world at large could not be trusted.

Thus I could not say, for example, how I longed to lie abed with him again, skin to skin, with the taste of him in my mouth. I could not say how I burned for him on those very long, very dark, very cold nights in the castle. I could not say how I craved the texture of his hair between my fingers, the heat of his body, or the bliss of his touch. You may imagine that I said all those things directly to him in the hours following our reunion.

Later that day (we had begun to put ourselves in order before going down for drinks with the Duchess) I wandered into Inigo's study and opened the box containing the scarlet knife. I'd spoken of it to the Marquess, as an item of interest during my consultation with the Duchess, then realized the intervening months had dimmed my recollection. I wanted to see it again.

Inigo joined me, knotting his tie. "Question?"

"Not really," I said absently, running a finger down the handle, enjoying the slippery bumps of the gems. "How did he give you this?"

He took my meaning. "Casually. We'd returned to the steamer from our time in India. Preparing to sail to New Zealand. Freddy wished to see the mud pots there. We were all in the private saloon opposite our cabins; he gave Fairchild a book and me this."

"Saying to you, it could be your security someday." I knew those were not the exact words, but close enough. This had been their last journey en famille; the Duke's horse went down within six months of their return to England.

He took up the knife. "It feels so awkward in my hand. Not like a dagger."

"No, it's made for hacking, not stabbing." We both laughed a bit. My attention was on the gems, gleaming in the late-afternoon light. He flourished the blade, circling his wrist. "Wait."

"Mmm?"

"Did you hear that?" He shook his head; repeated the movement; we both listened. There was a muffled sound, as of something loose inside the handle. "May I?" He passed it over; I took the thing closer to the window for better light, wishing I had brought my loupe this time. I carefully examined every aspect of the metalwork. Inigo was breathing down my neck; I turned my head with a smile, kissed him, and said, "I'd assumed the ornamented metal was wrapped around a lightweight wood handle into which the tang of the blade was sunk. But see." I took the flat of the blade between my fingers and manipulated it. It shifted up and down. "A working weapon would have a tang the length of the handle. This one may be quite short."

"Then is the handle hollow?" Our eyes met.

After a moment, burning with curiosity, I addressed the butt of the handle. The carved emerald there was set in a tightly-fitted cap. With another quick glance at Inigo (he nodded, giving permission) I pressed up with my thumbs, working the cap off. As it came free, he cupped his palm over it like the cork of a champagne bottle, gently twisting. A second later it came away. He set it on the desk with a cursory glance. "Yours," I said, handing him the knife again.

He tipped it up, blade flashing, and a two-carat cut diamond fell out. "Madre de Dios!" We were frozen in place for a moment. Then he sat down with a thump, nearly missing the desk chair, and put the tip of a finger up the handle. "Papers," he breathed. "And cotton?" Now he set the thing down, opened the desk drawer, and brought forth a pair of watchmaker's pliers. Inserted the long narrow jaws up the handle, closed them on something, and drew out a cylindrical bundle of paper wrapped around cotton. I watched as he tenderly straightened the paper. It proved to be a sheet of the Duke's notepaper, upon which was writ YOUR WORTH TO ME – A.F. Inigo audibly swallowed. Then he picked through the cotton. My arse landed on top of the desk as my knees gave way.

I have no sense of how long we were there, speechless, staring at the desk, before a knock came on the door. Inigo made a sound that was evidently construed as "Come in."

The hinges creaked apologetically; we heard Fairchild. "Are you not coming down? Good God! What is that?"

Well might she ask. The room was ablaze as the last rays of daylight shone across a king's ransom in diamonds.

"The stupid bugger," Fairchild said later, when we were downstairs making inroads on our second glasses of Scotch. "What if you'd sold it and never known?"

"Surely he meant to say something." The hand on Inigo's glass was still shaking a bit. I had the other clasped in mine. "There was some sort of crisis not long after we came home."

"There was always some sort of crisis. The family, the banks, the stock market, Parliament. Distractible, was Freddy," she told me.

"Busy," I corrected mildly, "with hundreds of dependents. Oh, Inigo, how he loved you."

He set down his glass hastily, strangling a sob. I put my arm around his shoulders, my own eyes wet, as he struggled for composure. Grimaced at Fairchild, who blinked hard, sniffed, and handed across her own handkerchief. Inigo mopped his face. Tried to apologize. We both shushed him. Eventually he said, "I might have given it to you, Duchess. Or to someone in my family. It might have been the great treasure of my estate, with that secret hid inside, until someone someday heard what Severin heard."

“Curious as a cat,” she murmured approvingly. “Well, should you care to, you could buy an entire village in Provence.”

Inigo coughed out a laugh. “And house all our inverted friends?”

“Why not?” She patted his knee. “I must write a letter for you, establishing provenance. Would you say those are Indian diamonds, Severin?”

I thought not; gems were cut somewhat differently in India. “More likely African. He must have been planning something for quite a while. He could not, surely, have acquired the lot at once.”

“Hmm. He went regularly to Antwerp for a period of time. Business, he said.” She shook her head. “Mendacity. But really, the stupid bugger! To bring those on board ship! Did he hide them in his shaving kit?!”

Inigo and I both laughed at the sheer incredulity in her tone. Then I changed the subject, away from the priceless handful we’d deposited in Fairchild’s safe; from the note, now tucked away with a few other such relics in Inigo’s locked trunk; and from the knife, now once more reposing in its box. Emerald cap in place, handle only slightly less weighty, a beautiful and ingenious storehouse for a man who could not fully own his love. Inigo need never even consider selling it.

My feelings were mixed. That I no longer brought the greater share of capital to our partnership was both a relief and – unexpectedly – an annoyance. I had rather liked the idea of being the man offering Inigo a future free of financial constraints. Between us, we would want for nothing. At least my contacts could be put to their best use in liquidating the diamonds, discreetly, over time.

And at least I could be the man offering him a future full of fearless love.

Inigo

September 1906

More than a year after I met Severin LaSalle, we were within sight of relocating to Provence. The village in which our friends (we could call them that, now) Agatha and Catriona resided comprised an abundance of appealing properties. We chose to acquire a modest tavern, converting the ground floor to a café with poste restante; the previous keeper and her adult children would manage it. The upper floor would be our dwelling, with two bedrooms, two offices, a modern washroom, a library, and a sunroom overlooking a walled garden. Upon inquiry, I had been informed that, in view of the current schoolmaster's imminent retirement, my services would be welcome. Once upon a time I had wished for children of my own; instead, my legacy would be a clutch of French boys and girls. It was enough.

Severin seemed to be constantly traveling, either on our business or on that of the Marquess. He was in France when our friend and solicitor Donald Richards married; he had but recently returned when Fairchild and Elizabeth went to visit Donald and his wife at their new estate near Leicester. After a thorough and robust reunion, he showed me the artwork Catriona had produced. Engravings would be made, illustrations for the publication of his great-grandsire's memoir.

We were yet disinclined to leave my rooms when a footman delivered a telegram from Fairchild. "From Birmingham," I said, puzzled. "She says Donald has need of your expertise. Something about dragons."

Severin snorted a laugh into the knit jumper he was tugging over his head. "We could go once she's returned."

I hid my smile at that. There would be other opportunities to enjoy our friends en masse; for now, taking them two or three at a time was sufficient. "Shall I wire him to that effect?"

"Certainly." He then came to me and made it quite impossible for me to do anything useful.

Upon the return of Fairchild, Elizabeth, et al., we had several pleasantly social evenings. Fairchild had clearly mixed feelings about my imminent removal to France; we had, after all, lived together a long time. She hid it well, telling us a treat was in store in the Midlands. Elizabeth told us that she meant to convert a small room in her house to a washroom with a soaking tub like the one at Donald's house. "With any luck, Ashvi can oversee that while Fairchild and I and the boys are on our trip."

"What trip?"

"India!" she said excitedly. "The Taj Mahal!"

"If there is any business I can assist with, Severin, do brief me," Fairchild said. "Unless you intend to visit your family soon?"

"Not within the next year," he said. "Thank you, I'll look into it."

We then talked at length about India, or rather the others talked at length while I listened indulgently. Elizabeth was nearly twenty years Severin's junior, as Fairchild was nearly twenty years mine; we both may be forgiven a somewhat avuncular approach to the ladies. They did not seem to mind, at any rate.

A few days later, we had dinner with Marius and Sunnam at the Equatorial Club. Sunnam was almost as excited about the India voyage as Elizabeth. Marius, decidedly less so, as his previous experience with ocean travel was limited to an Atlantic crossing. I assured him that travel down the European coast, through the Mediterranean and the Suez Canal, and across the Indian Ocean was not like to be as challenging. He gave me a skeptical look and began listing the various hazards. Sunnam interrupted to remind him of Fairchild's promise regarding a coastal route. We left them still bickering, and laughed about it most of the next day as we traveled to Leicestershire.

A hired carriage delivered us to the Richards manor on a glowing autumn afternoon. The air was redolent of apples, which Donald's wife Aurelia explained first thing. "Our cider house is running full time," she said, showing us up to our adjoining rooms. "By this time next year, we hope to have a license to distill apple brandy." Severin made an appreciative sound; she gave him a happy nod. "Your travel was comfortable? Please ring for anything you need, and come down whenever you like. I'll be in the music room and Donald is in the study."

"Thank you, my dear," I said. "What a very appealing house this is."

"Isn't it? We are so *very* lucky." She smiled brightly and went out.

"Surely she knows we do not require two rooms," Severin murmured, amused.

"It is a genteel fiction," I agreed, just as softly. "If the household was not shaken by Fairchild, Elizabeth, Marius, and Sunnam, I doubt we will create a disturbance."

So it proved over the next few days. Our purpose there was singular: to identify, catalogue, and give a preliminary valuation on the collection of gemstones hidden away by the previous owner. The property had descended to Donald almost by chance, a many-branched family having dwindled to a single twig. Half our time was spent roaming the grounds, listening to Aurelia or Donald talk, and relating to them the similarly vast changes on our own horizon. The other half was spent in the study. I had by now a good working knowledge of gemology (one cannot be in the same room with Severin and Elizabeth and fail to absorb the substance of their conversation), so I performed the first round. There were things that baffled me, however. Those cases became enjoyable lectures, Severin holding forth with his magnifying glasses, Mohs kit, scales, etc. while the rest of us listened.

"This is, one might say, a nice bit of rough," he said, handing over an uncut crystal of deep blue. Donald and I both snorted; Aurelia stifled a laugh while trying to frown at us, which meant she knew the term had a salacious connotation, which meant our friends had already thoroughly corrupted her. "Hold the crystal in front of the window, Aurelia, where the sun comes through." She did; we all crooned over the violet color that resulted. "Now turn it forty-five degrees to the right, and tilt it forty-five degrees posterior." We all exclaimed at the green flash. Another turn, another tilt, and it flashed red. "This is alexandrite, from Russia," he said, pleased by the effect of the demonstration. "It's uncommon and will, I think, one day be much prized. Nearly impossible to match stones, however, so you may wish to set it individually."

Aurelia made a note on a bit of card, handing it and the stone back to Donald. He placed them in the drawer, then passed one more thing to Severin. "This looks like nothing more than a greasy gray pebble," he said. "But the old master wouldn't've kept it on a whim."

"All the gods," Severin said, staring blankly at the chunk of crystal. We made inquiring noises.

From my point of view, the best that could be said was that the thing had an interesting shape, as of two pyramids set base to base. In the back of my mind I thought there was some significance to that, but I could not recall precisely what. Thus I was full of expectation as we watched him measure and weigh it, scrape it on a specimen from his Mohs kit, and take it to the window. He made a high-pitched sound. At length I said, "What is it?"

Severin returned to our group, handed the crystal to Aurelia, and said, "Did you hear of the blue diamond Lord Hope sold five years ago?

She sucked in a breath. "No!" Obviously she did not mean she hadn't heard of it. "But it isn't blue!"

"It will be," he said.

That was the last of it. We left Mr. and Mrs. Richards to determine how to handle their dragons' hoard (each locked drawer of gemstones was guarded by a taxidermy chimera; quite a startling effect). Severin of course offered his assistance when and if they should decide to sell off, cut, or set any of the collection.

We also offered our spare bedroom should they find themselves in Provence. "We'll be on our way next month," I said, hardly believing it. "Must get settled. I take up my duties as schoolmaster in January."

Aurelia embraced each of us, kissing our cheeks. "I wish you as much joy of your new home as we've found here."

“We could hardly ask for more,” Severin said with a smile. We shook hands with Donald, climbed into the waiting coach, and were on our way.

Of course our Oxford friends wanted to know everything about the dragons’ hoard. Elizabeth asked after a particular sapphire; Severin told her it still reposed in the drawer with the others. Donald had scribbled ‘for my love’ on the bit of card that lay beneath it. “She’ll write their story,” I said, leaning comfortably back in my chair.

Marius said, “Meaning Aurelia, about the old master and his preserver?”

“Yes, sorry. We read bits of the manuscript while we were there.”

“I’m almost surprised they let you handle it.” Sunnam was leaning forward, elbows on the table, smiling.

“Sworn to secrecy and denied any food or beverage, lest we mar the pages,” Severin said. “It was inspiring.”

I lifted a hand, resting it on the back of his chair where my thumb could brush his shoulder. “My travels with the Duke were nothing in comparison,” I admitted. “And yet I thought each of our voyages such a great adventure.”

Elizabeth said, “They *were* great adventures! Imagine how few people ever leave their country of birth! There you were, crossing the oceans to see countries you’d only read about.” Her excitement about their upcoming expedition was clear. As were the facts that Sunnam still eagerly anticipated the voyage, while Marius was resigned to it. We all make compromises for love.

Smiling at the thought, I said, "I only went adventuring because of Freddy. To grow tomatoes in Provence is more to my liking. To sit in the sun with a glass of wine, a field of lavender at my back." And the man I loved by my side.

Perhaps Severin heard those unspoken words. He turned his head, looked at me, and smiled.

Severin

Was it a happy ending of fairy-tale perfection? Of course not. There were travel delays, misplaced luggage, fiendishly bad weather, and a leaking roof. There were also dozens of letters from England, Ceylon, and Spain, as everyone who knew us demanded news. We had a skirmish with a farmer over the unreliable supply of chèvre (which both of us considered essential to life); we battled a sturdy and implacable tomcat who would not be ejected from the garden.

In time we mended the roof, answered all the letters, pacified the farmer, and surrendered to the cat.

Meanwhile we worked, dined, slept, and rose together every day. It was a dream of love no less blissful for its imperfections. And this should be our life, the best of it, for all the rest of it.

On the last day of the year I looked across my office at Inigo, sprawled in a chair before the fire, frowning handsomely at a Latin text he would, in a week's time, bravely attempt to impart to his pupils. He must have felt my gaze; he looked up and smiled. "Je t'aime," he said.

"Te amo también," I said, with all my heart.

THE END

Of

The Scarlet Knife

Read on for

LAVENDER FIELDS

Severin

August 1907

I laid aside the latest from Elizabeth – she and Fairchild had left Russia behind and were en route to Denmark – and looked around for Inigo. This being midday of midweek of a month during which Europeans departed en masse from their places of business and descended en masse upon places of leisure, the village was plagued with holidaymakers. We both, therefore, concealed ourselves in the garden for most of any given day. 'Concealed' being the operative term; said garden was extensive. Inigo was not in sight. I set a Murano glass paperweight on top of my stack of letters, got to my feet, and went to find him.

Then I turned on my heel and went back to find Javert (the cat) in the act of shoving the paperweight aside. I swore at him, snatched up the letters, and crammed them into my various pockets. He gave me an arrogant look. "Be damned to you, nefarious beast," I said, walking away.

The original walled courtyard, which had previously accommodated drinkers and smokers overflowing from the tavern, provided a border of roses, a whimsical fountain, a pergola covered with hops vines (beneath which I'd been reading), and a pollarded almond tree. We'd knocked through the back wall so this tree could gossip unimpeded with its fellows on the other side.

Between the hops, the roses, and the neighboring fields of lavender, our garden continuously hummed with bees. I'd been shy of them in the beginning, and inclined to be offended the first time I was stung. Then

I noticed that my hands (aged beyond my years by work in the gem gravel) grew less stiff and painful. I did not precisely invite stings, but I ceased to flail and curse when a bee landed on me. One rode on my sleeve as I walked, its fur glinting gold in the sun.

An improved path wound through the orchard to a stream. Along the way were various arbors which would, in time, support grapevines. These were yet adolescent and resisting all attempts at training. Beneath these arbors were benches, and I expected to find my husband (for so we thought of each other) on one of them. Not even the dottle from his pipe did I see.

Eventually I found him, at the very end, where our land abutted that of the Fletchers. The neighboring farmers had sold their interest; they remained to manage the house and garden, but Agatha was now ruler of her domain. While Catriona made a name for herself as an illustrator (her paintings for my ancestor's memoir led to several other commissions, including plates for a book about two gentleman travelers), Agatha embarked on a new venture of beekeeping. If you have never had fresh bread with chèvre and honey, please accept my sympathies.

Inigo sat under an oak tree, on a wrought-iron settee with Catriona, his arms full of the plump infant recently delivered by our friend Aurelia. The mother lay on the grass in the sun, smiling at something. Perhaps at her husband Donald, who was a short distance away with Agatha and a certain goat she'd made a pet of.

Catriona was sketching, as usual. Inigo watched her, but must have noticed my approach; he glanced up and smiled at me. Said something to her. She glanced up too, waving. I walked up the path to join them.

Inigo

In other times, and other places, I would have hesitated; but here on the sunny hillside within sight of our home, when Aurelia offered her child to me I could not resist. “In my youth I was said to be good with children,” I said as the infant settled contentedly against me. “But I suspect that was merely flattery to secure my child-minding services.”

“Both things might have been true,” she pointed out as she subsided to the ground (aided by her husband’s arm). “Ah, God, the sun feels good.” They murmured together, too low for me to hear, before Donald wandered off to join Agatha and her goat.

We were all quiet then for a while. Catriona was sketching, as usual; Aurelia lay on the grass like a sated Bacchante; and I cradled our friends’ precious child. Who would have guessed that a village in Provence would deliver unto this vagrant Spaniard the most paternal experiences I could wish?

I was not to remain the village schoolmaster. I’d merely served out the previous term while the townsmen conducted a search for a new, younger, French educator. That man was now arrived and settling in. He’d made a point of calling on me to ask if he might benefit from my counsel. Of course I said he was welcome to whatever counsel I could provide. I’d made a point of offering assistance on days he might be unwell, or required to be away. Meanwhile those few months’ service had rendered me, in the eyes of the local parents, a sort of honorary uncle. I’d even stood godfather to a new son of the local brewer. Our life here was a full one.

In the distance I could see, along the road, a pair of our neighbors, traveling at a smart clip on dusty brown horses. Closer to I could see, along the path leading to this oak tree, Severin. He could be relied on to come and find me if we were apart more than a few hours. "Here he is," I said, speaking as much to the baby as to Catriona.

It was Catriona who answered. "Good God, he suits this setting." She turned over a leaf of her sketchbook and laid down a few quick lines. The broad-brimmed hat; the open-necked shirt with sleeves rolled up; the Madras silk waistcoat over blue linen trousers. The sharp bones of his face, the fine eyes, the bright smile.

"The only thing lacking in this picture is a picnic basket," he said as he approached.

"We were, in fact, just discussing that," Catriona said. "The proposal was that Inigo – and you, now you've joined us – could come back to ours for lunch."

"Donald appears to be considering bees," I told Severin. He laid a hand on my shoulder; I turned my head to touch my cheek to his forearm.

Then he was bending near, crouching to touch the baby's tiny nose with his fingertip. It squinted blearily at him, wriggled, yawned, and resumed sleeping. "What a pretty child."

"It is, isn't it?" Aurelia, still lying on the grass, sounded lazily proud. "We're hoping for Donald's eyes and my hair." We all snickered.

Donald

"Oi! Get off!" I pushed ineffectually at the head of Agatha's goat, which was again attempting to eat the hem of my jacket. "Can you not leash this beast?"

"It's a goat, Donald," she said in a derisive tone. "It would eat through anything but chain."

I huffed at her, at the goat, at the situation. Stepped away, glared at the goat's Satanic eyes, and waited to see which of us would win the staring contest. Because goats have a short attention span, I won. Once it wandered off I turned to Agatha again. "You've convinced me. I'll find a local expert and inquire as to the best time to bring in some hives."

"With all those apple trees, you'll have more honey than you can use." She glanced over at the group beneath the oak tree. "Aurelia looks well."

"She's resisted all her friends' advice to lie slothfully about the house," I said proudly. "Out in the garden two days after delivering Draco."

"You're not really calling him that, are you?"

Of course we were. We'd a selection of names for the boy to choose from once he reached an age to do so: Orel Marlais Draco Richards. It was a nine months' labor to whittle the male half of the list down to Golden Blue Dragon, given the over-educated multilingual featherheads who were our friends. (Our Indian friends nearly took offense at our choosing the Latin for dragon, but were eventually pacified.) I glanced at Agatha and smiled. "It was the one name that consistently topped the rankings."

"Catriona wondered if you would try for another child right away."

"Not to say try," I hedged. "We were a bit surprised by the, er, promptness of this one." She laughed. Started to say something, laughed again, and finally walked away for a moment. I heard her blow out a shaky breath. There was no doubt Aurelia and I had taken to procreation as if made for it. We told each other it was proof of how well we suited. We then looked at the calendar, because if we could expect that to happen again we might have some influence over the timing; a second delivery could be, if not precisely scheduled, at least optimized. We were by now experts in pleasing each other in ways that were less likely to, shall we say, accelerate the schedule. When at length Agatha joined me again, I said, "Ideally a second child could also be born in the summer."

"Ah. Well thought of. We are planning to adopt."

"Are you? Excellent! Is there a local child of interest?"

"A painter friend of Cat's, in Paris, knows of a boy who'd be best off in the country. Six years old."

"A good age for a change of residence. And you've a family ready-made for him here."

"Mmm." We both stood there, gazing out over the lavender field. The scent of it was nearly overpowering. "Oh, hello."

I turned to see who Agatha greeted; it was a honeybee, crawling on her cuff. She lifted her hand as if to make eye contact with the insect. Then she jolted; the goat had butted her hip; the bee flew away. "Your goat is no respecter of persons," I said.

"Goats never are." We were both smiling as we returned to the others.

Aurelia

Donald and Agatha gave me their hands, helping me to my feet. I was in most ways recovered from childbirth, but from recumbent to upright still took effort. By the end of the summer I intended to be walking and riding as easily as I'd done last year. There was no doubt, in my mind, that activity and my health were linked.

I was prepared to argue that happiness and mental challenge kept us well, too. Donald continued to serve his clients, riding three days a week to Coventry for office hours; I had undertaken to edit the memoir left by the old master. Once I'd written out a copy of the passages that would not betray his relationship with the preserver, I'd begun to build the in-between through the other records he'd left. The letters, the detritus of travel, and the bills of lading: a single trunk might have contained half a dozen books, a chest of geological specimens, a piece of native art, and a sheaf of the preserver's sketches, each with a story to it.

Then I'd read through my workmanlike assembly and seen other gaps, which required research into the countries where the two men had traveled; other Europeans they'd encountered; their modes of transportation; and historical events coinciding with their presence in a given locale. It was a tremendous education.

I had at first thought to illustrate the book purely with the preserver's sketches, but Donald wanted color plates of the dragons. We'd thus secured photographs of the chimerae and written out detailed descriptions of the colors and textures for Catriona. She also drew maps for us, in a whimsical style including sketches of flora and fauna. One day, I told Donald, we could use this book to educate our children.

As we meandered toward the farmhouse, I edged closer to Catriona. "My thanks again for putting us up. This is the perfect place to recover."

"I found it so," she agreed. "I'd never have thought that I could feel better after three months of winter in Provence than after three of summer in London."

"I have not missed London for a day. Perhaps by the time we travel home I'll be happy to spend some time there."

"Where will you stay?"

"My brother has a house now," I said. "In a terrace not far from Donald's friend Walpole. A week there should dispose of our social obligations."

"And you can refresh your wardrobe."

"Indeed," I said with feeling. What with one thing and another, I'd dressed myself piecemeal for years. After the private sale (arranged by Severin) of a selection of the old master's gemstones, we could well afford to kit me out in a much more intentional manner. "Shall we send you a few bottles of the new cider?"

"Bien sûr. Do you distill this year?"

I squeaked with excitement. "We do! Our man Morris went to take training in Scotland and in Caen. He'd never been to France before."

"Did he like it?"

I glanced over; Catriona was smiling. "He's so bloody English, pet. He came home complaining that everyone talked French at him all the time." She laughed. I grinned back at her. "Then he made some jingoistic statements to the effect that our apple brandy would be better than theirs. His cider is a marvel, so we haven't argued the point. Fairchild has demanded the first bottle."

"She would."

Fairchild

I was never in doubt that Elizabeth would swoon at Elsinore. She had not at first believed it was a real place; when I pointed out that Verona and Venice were real places she blinked at me, produced an impatient sigh, and dove into Shakespeare. In very little time she was satisfied that most of his settings were actual, not fictional.

We'd been several months looping through Europe, alternating adventurous excursions for me (the Alps, etc) with cultural submersion for her (Rome, etc). Having extended the definition of 'Europe' to include Moscow and St. Petersburg, we were now en route from Denmark to Norway. Elizabeth would soon be on her way home to Oxford via Scotland; I was going on to Iceland.

On this particular tour we were accompanied only by the former housemaid Mary. She'd been such a success as our travel attendant on last winter's steamer trip to Ceylon, we'd all felt quite comfortable doing without Marius this time. He and Sunnam were, according to their letters, spending what should have been their leisure time overhauling Elizabeth's library.

Sunnam was also in charge of my correspondence these days. Losing Inigo to Provence had produced barely a hiccup in my business. We'd stopped at the village for several days, ostensibly to leave christening gifts for Donald and Aurelia. In fact it was a chance for us to satisfy ourselves that Agatha and Catriona were happy, and that Severin and Inigo had no regrets. The latter two had attempted to foist their occupying cat upon us. Apparently they made this attempt with everyone they knew.

Our itinerary being known to our friends, there were letters waiting for us in Gothenburg. Once settled into our rooms, we each had a stretch of time alone. This was part of our routine, since Elizabeth well knew I needed a regular dose of solitude. I stood by my window, staring out at the lingering light of a far-north summer evening, imagining I could see all the way to Orkney.

Elizabeth had considered coming along to Iceland, but there was as yet no university there, and volcano trekking did not appeal. This would be our lengthiest separation to date; a test, perhaps, of our bond. Either that or, as she said, a palate cleanser. The thought made me smile.

After an hour alone, I rang for tea. We would dine in Elizabeth's room later. For now, I sat down at the writing desk and composed a letter, because I knew how my love treasured them.

Dear Lizzie,

Should you ever wonder if I would prefer a different traveling companion, let me assure you that nothing could be further from the truth.

You help me see things. Your enthusiasm for every new experience (even the frustration of negotiating Customs at the Russian border!) is endlessly refreshing.

I viewed travel differently with Freddy, and with Caroline. Now I imagine returning to past destinations with you at my side, and I know it will be like seeing those places for the first time. How many people can say they have seen the world even once?

Now I will see it all, even the places we visit only in the pages of books, anew.

I shall always be thankful that of all the people you might have crossed an ocean to meet, you chose me.

Ever yours,

G.F.

Elizabeth

"Thank you, Mary," I said distractedly. She dropped the lid of my trunk with a thump. "What?"

"Nothing, miss."

I finished sorting through the letters held for us at the hotel. "Ah, *here* it is." I handed her the envelope with 'Darley' scrawled in the corner. "Sam's written you again."

I will not say that she snatched it from my hand, but she certainly removed it with alacrity. I stifled a laugh. She gave me a half-apologetic look as I handed her the letter knife. "Thanks, miss."

"You're very welcome." I turned my attention to the letter from Marius. He and Sunnam were splitting their time between my house and Fairchild's, and they were making the most of their lengthy holiday. After all these years, I could read between Marius' lines *very* well.

My dresser Daisy had, he said, decamped entirely. She and Fairchild's woman Polly were bosom friends now (at least). Daisy's own letter reported an excursion for both of them to London, involving a stay at the Boudica and a week of theatre-going. Polly's many theatrical friends in the city were still celebrating the success of last winter's strike for better pay and working conditions.

"I may not get Daisy back," I mused aloud.

"What's that, miss?"

"Daisy and Polly are in London and loving it. D'you think the Duchess and I should set them up in lodgings? We could find new help for all that." I waved a hand at the open wardrobe, where my traveling clothes now hung to air and relax. Much as I did in a light wrapper from Kashmir.

"Ashvi and I could train a new girl for you," Mary suggested. "If you want to go to the trouble."

"Mmm. I can't imagine a person of Daisy's qualities being content as my tirewoman forever." There was a clicking sound from across the room, which I had no doubt was accompanied by rolling eyes. I swiveled around to stare at Mary. "Well, you were ambitious enough; why should she not be?"

She set down her letter. It did not escape my notice that she smoothed it lovingly. She and my driver Sam had been circling each other like a pair of wary cats since I'd hired them on; only recently had I observed the advent of warmer feelings. She cleared her throat. "Of course, you're right, miss. Wouldn't you miss her, though?"

"Naturally I would. But London and Oxford are no great distance." And I had others to meet my needs. In truth, I'd barely missed Daisy since she left my bed for Polly's. In the physical sense, that is. I'd miss her sorely did she leave my house entirely.

But we were, as we all promised each other, devoted to our *mutual* happiness. That sometimes meant letting someone go. Now that I was mistress of my own home and fate, I'd come to enjoy the occasional night alone. As long as I had Marius and Fairchild, I'd little need for another.

There came a tap on the door. Mary opened it; accepted something; assured the giver that tea would be very welcome. Then she brought me a note, folded over and sealed with Fairchild's wafer. "From the Duchess, miss."

"Ooh!" A moment later I'd read it, and I was dabbing discreetly at my eyes, then reaching for my own notepaper. A quick line or two only, because we'd see each other at dinner, but I knew how my love treasured my letters.

Dear George,

There is no one alive with whom I'd rather see the world. Isn't it marvelous? There's so much left!

Ever yours,

E.B.

THE END

By the same author:

Nonfiction
Other Voices: Social Commentary in the Novels of Frances Burney

Regency M/M/M Romance
The Hunting Box

*****

About the Author

A.Y. Caluen is the award-winning author of over sixty romance novels, novellas and short stories featuring diverse, creative professionals. Her settings range from Los Angeles to London, North Carolina to New York. Alexandra is the human servant of a tabby cat, loves wine country, has been known to break into a song or dance, and once performed in the Tournament of Roses Parade.

Connect with me:

Queeromance Ink: Alexandra Caluen

Follow me on Instagram: @the.l.a.stories

Subscribe to my blog: http://thelastories.com

www.ingramcontent.com/pod-product-compliance
Lightning Source LLC
La Vergne TN
LVHW091312150826
845673LV00006B/1624

* 9 7 9 8 9 8 5 6 3 1 8 5 2 *